THE FOSTER
HOUSE

First paperback edition October 2023
Revised edition March 2026

Cover design by Alex Albornoz

ISBN 9798855609738

https://csmithauthor.wixsite.com/author

THE FOSTER
HOUSE

C. SMITH

"The boundaries which divide Life from Death are at best shadowy and vague."
— Edgar Allan Poe

CHAPTER ONE

"Finally!" I shouted, reaching toward the ceiling like I'd just won an Oscar—except my audience was my empty bedroom.

Two days of editing hours upon hours of audio and camera footage had left me absolutely drained, but my latest paranormal investigation was finally ready to upload to YouTube for the world to see. I glanced at the clock on my laptop screen. Nearly eight at night. No wonder my eyelids felt like someone had hooked dumbbells to them.

I'd barely gotten out of my gaming chair when my laptop made a *ding!* alerting me to a new email. I glanced at the pile of memory foam pillows and cozy blankets that covered my bed like a fluffy cloud, longing to burrow into them for the night. I almost did just that, but something clenched in my gut, giving an urgent warning I couldn't ignore.

With a groan, I sat back down and clicked on the email.

Good evening Ava,

I've been a fan of your channel for a long time, and I'm hoping you might be able to help me. My dad took over our family's old bed-and-breakfast. Ever since we reopened in January, strange things have been happening. Weird shadows, objects moving, the usual. But what really bothers me is my dad. He's not himself anymore. I'm scared he might be possessed.

The last line made my stomach twist. In the five years I'd been a paranormal investigator, I had only dealt with one possession case. It didn't end well. The thought of taking on that challenge again scared the living crap out of me.

But you can't let another family suffer either, my conscience whispered. God, I hated that thing sometimes—especially when it was right.

I closed my eyes, inhaled deeply, then exhaled. If this truly was another possession, I had to try to help them. I couldn't—no, I *wouldn't*—make the same mistake again.

The email was signed *Samantha Foster*. Under her name was a phone number with an unfamiliar area code. No name of the bed-and-breakfast and no location was given.

Even though I wanted nothing more than to sleep, I grabbed my cellphone and dialed the number.

Brrring… Brrring… Brrring…

A rustling sound came over the line, like the phone had been answered from inside someone's pocket. Then silence as the call dropped.

"That's weird," I muttered before dialing again.

Brrring… Brrring… Brrring…

More rustling and another dead line.

I had gotten prank messages before asking for help with a fake haunting and receiving a dead-end number. But something nudged me to try one more time.

"Thank you for calling The Foster House," an overly perky voice answered after the first ring. "This is Samantha speaking."

"Hi Samantha. This is Ava Moore. I just got your email and wanted to talk with you about your situation."

Her cheerfulness vanished instantly. "Thank you for getting back to me," she whispered.

"I'm always happy to help." Then I cut to the chase. "Do you know what's causing the paranormal phenomena?"

There was a long pause before she said, "I'm not sure. A ghost or a demon maybe? Things just aren't… *normal* around here."

"Not normal as in your dad possibly being possessed."

It wasn't a question, but she answered anyway. "Yes. But I can't talk about that right now." Her words tumbled out quickly, like she was eager to change the subject before someone overheard it.

Maybe she doesn't feel safe.

"What did you say the name of the place is?" I asked. She had said it when she first answered the phone, but my brain occasionally went full Dory, and some bits of information just go *poof!*

"The Foster House."

A quick Google search showed it sat in a small town just outside Little Rock, Arkansas. Over four hours from my apartment in Tulsa, Oklahoma. I usually didn't travel out of state for solo cases.

"It's a little far," I said carefully.

"I'll pay extra to cover the travel costs," Samantha offered quickly. "And you can stay here. Room and meals on the house."

I chewed the inside of my cheek, running a hand through my messy blond hair. She sounded genuinely scared about whatever was going on there. But what if I drove all that way for a prank? Or worse—what if her dad *was* possessed and I was too far to call for backup?

"Before I agree," I said, "I'd like to speak to your dad."

The line went silent, long enough that I pulled my phone away to check the screen, just to make sure we hadn't been disconnected. "Samantha?"

"Hang on," she murmured. "I'll transfer you to his room."

Lame elevator music blared in my ear while I waited. Then a gruff voice answered.

"This is Mike Foster."

"Hi Mike," I replied, keeping my tone professional. "My name is Ava Moore. Your daughter contacted me about some unusual activity. Have you noticed anything strange yourself?"

He let out a short, humorless laugh. "I apologize for her bothering you. My daughter has quite the imagination."

"So there's nothing unusual happening?"

"Business has been slow, but that's typical for this time of year."

I frowned, annoyed that he wouldn't give me a straight answer. "Do you know why it's been slow?"

"She scares everyone away." His voice had turned flat.

"Who? Samantha?" Static began to flood the line. "Mike? Are you there?"

His reply was muffled. "She's messing with the phone."

"Who are you talking about?" I pressed.

His response was drowned out by a surge of static so intense I half expected a little girl's voice to whisper, *they're here.*

"What?" I shouted into the phone.

This must be the weird stuff Samantha was talking about.

"I have to go," Mike said abruptly as the static faded slightly.

"Why? Who's there?" My heart pounded with a surge of adrenaline.

"No one."

I held my breath, listening intently. A door slammed in the background. Then heavy breathing replaced the static.

"Mike?" I asked carefully. "What's happening?"

When he spoke, his voice was ice. "She's here."

A shiver crawled up my spine, and I sat up straighter in my chair. From somewhere around Mike came the faint, unmistakable sound of a young woman giggling.

And just like that, the line went dead.

CHAPTER TWO

I stared at the phone in my trembling hand as if it were a ticking bomb counting down to zero. What the hell just happened? After a few slow, steady breaths, my heart rate finally returned to normal.

Grabbing one of my millions of notebooks, I scribbled everything I remembered from the call while it was still fresh in my mind. The more I wrote, the more bizarre it all sounded. Something was definitely off with Mike, but was it possession? The call alone was not enough to confirm that. But one thing was abundantly clear: Samantha and Mike needed my help.

I turned back to my laptop, reopened Samantha's email, and hit reply.

Hi Samantha,

Yes, I will help you. I'll head your way first thing tomorrow morning. If you need anything before then, give me a call.

After adding my signature block, I clicked send, closed the laptop, and started packing. Since I had no idea how long I would be gone, I crammed roughly a week's worth of clothes into my duffel bag, rolling each piece tight—a little packing trick I learned years ago.

In the corner of my bedroom sat my paranormal investigation equipment, all charged and ready for their next adventure. As I secured each item in their respective carrying case, I couldn't help noticing how outdated most of it had become. That should've been the least of my worries, but it was a nice distraction from thinking about what tomorrow would bring me.

When everything was packed and ready, I checked my phone. It was almost ten thirty. Part of me wanted to start digging into the history of The Foster House, but the other part knew I needed to hit the hay.

Sleep should have come easily with how exhausted I was, but my mind kept wandering back to the new case, stirring up fresh waves of anxiety. After what felt like hours of trying to get comfortable, I sat up and picked up my phone from the nightstand. There was only one person who could ease my worries: Austin Reed.

Austin and I had met three years ago when we were each called by two separate people to investigate an abandoned building near Oklahoma City. We clicked instantly and have been best friends ever since. And yes—I'd had a crush on him from the moment we met. Does he know? Absolutely not. Confessing my feelings might ruin everything, and I couldn't risk losing him.

I unlocked my phone and sent him a text.

`Are you awake?`

His reply came almost immediately.

`Of course. What's up?`

I hesitated. I wanted him to calm me down, but I couldn't tell him why my nerves were wound up so tight to begin with. If I mentioned the case, he'd either try to talk me out of it or insist on coming along. He'd grown protective of me over time—way more than I'd expected.

Then my phone rang, blasting a song by Savage Garden I'd set as his ringtone. He already knew something was wrong.

I couldn't help but smile as I answered the call. "Hey."

"Hey." Austin's voice, deep but gentle, melted my nerves in an instant. "You okay?"

Even though he couldn't see it, I shrugged. "Yeah, I'm fine."

"You're lying."

Completely ignoring his truthful accusation, I leaned back against my pillows and asked lightly, "Hey, have you ever heard of The Foster House?"

He paused for a moment before answering, "No, I don't think so. Why?"

"Well, I just accepted a new case there."

"Where is it?"

"Just outside of Little Rock."

"Arkansas?" Concern was clear in his voice, and I knew his protective side was about to take over. "That's a little far to go alone. Maybe I should come with you."

Called it. Still, his offer made me all tingly inside. "Thanks, but I can handle it on my own. It'll be a fun little adventure."

"Okay." Just that single word was weighed down with disappointment.

I didn't want to worry him further, but he was the only person who could answer my next question. "Have you ever had a weird phone call when getting information about a case?"

"Define *weird*."

"You know, like lots of static, a person saying off the wall things, calls dropping," I listed.

"No, not really." He fell silent for a moment, thinking. "Wait—are you talking about this Arkansas case?"

"Well, yeah but—"

"What do you know about the place?" he cut in.

"Nothing really," I admitted, a little sheepishly. "Just, you know, shadows and objects moving on their own—the usual." I totally wasn't planning to say this next part, but my stupid mouth had other ideas. "Oh, and the owner might be possessed."

I heard him mutter something under his breath before he said, "Let me come with you. You don't have to do this alone again, babe."

"What?" My jaw dropped. *Did he just…?* No way. I had to be hearing things—which, given the night I'd had, wouldn't have been surprising.

"Ava," he corrected himself a little too quickly, then cleared his throat—something he does when things get awkward. "Look, I just feel like you're getting in way over your head again."

"No I'm not." I tried to sound confident—*tried*. "I know more now than I did back then."

"Ava, please don't do this."

"I'm taking the case, Austin. I have to."

I put extra emphasis on the last part, hoping he'd understand what this meant for me. It would be my way of making up for my past mistake.

"You can't help everyone. Stop blaming yourself for what happened."

I wanted to shout my frustrations at him, but I kept my voice calm. "I'll be fine. I've got this. Really."

"Okay," he said reluctantly, the worry still clear in his tone. "Just promise you'll call if you need me, okay?"

"I promise."

He let out a soft sigh of relief. "Goodnight, Ava."

"Goodnight."

I set my phone on the nightstand and burrowed under the blankets. Austin was right—I was getting in way over my head. It would've been so easy to let him come along, but my intuition was telling me I had to do this on my own. Why? The question lingered in my mind for only a moment before sleep claimed me.

CHAPTER THREE

Asia's *Heat of the Moment* blared beside my head, rudely ending my dream of stealing cupcakes from a bakery. Groaning, I rolled over and silenced my alarm. I lay there for a moment longer before forcing myself to get up and ready for the long day ahead.

The drive to Arkansas went by surprisingly fast, and before I knew it, my GPS alerted me that my destination was a quarter mile away. My eyes flicked to the dashboard—two fifteen in the afternoon. I'd have plenty of time to get settled in and start the investigation before the day was over.

The Foster House sat in a secluded area just outside of town. A stone wall, varying in shades of gray, lined the property along the road. The large wrought-iron gate at the entrance stood wide open, allowing guests to come and go freely. Tall oak trees filled the space beyond the wall, shrouding my view of the place like it was harboring a secret from the world.

I steered my Tahoe onto the gravel driveway that led toward the building. The second I crossed the property line, I felt a strong, eerie presence settle around me. It made the hairs on the nape of my neck stand on end.

I didn't know who or what it was yet, but it definitely wasn't Casper the Friendly Ghost.

Pushing my uneasy feeling aside, I stared in awe as the building came into view; surrounded by a vast, dense forest. The Georgian-style bed and breakfast stood two stories tall and built of red brick that had begun to fade over the years. Vines had sprouted and crawled their way up the walls in a beautifully unorganized fashion. Tall windows with black shutters adorned the front of the building. A small flower bed near the front door overflowed with purple and white blossoms. In it stood a wood sign that read *The Foster House* in a large, elegant font.

The driveway opened into a small gravel parking lot. Only two other vehicles were—presumably belonging to Sam and Mike. I pulled into an unmarked spot and cut the engine. After grabbing my bags from the trunk, I headed for the entrance, aware of the unsettling sensation of being watched. It's normal to feel that way on a case, but this time was different: more intense and impossible to ignore.

I pushed open the heavy wooden door and stepped inside.

The interior was breathtakingly beautiful, but the invisible presence was stronger now—almost sinister. To my left was a common area that had a red antique sofa facing a brick fireplace. A wooden bookcase filled with books that looked older than me stood along a wall between two windows that faced the woods outside. An ancient grandfather clock sat between the door I'd come in through and another window overlooking the parking lot.

To my right, an archway led into what appeared to be a guest dining room. From where I stood, I could make out a couple of round tables covered in beige tablecloths with four wooden chairs at each one. I wondered how long it had been since any guests had actually eaten there.

Straight ahead was the front desk, a gigantic crystal chandelier hanging above it from the high ceiling. A girl who looked around my age—early twenties—stood behind the desk, engrossed in a stack of papers. The sound of the door shutting behind me and the old wooden floor creaking beneath my feet as I walked caught her attention. Her head snapped up. For a split second, her body went rigid, terror flashing in her eyes. Then, just as quickly, she relaxed.

"Hi Ava," she greeted me with a warm smile.

"Hey," I replied, matching her friendliness. "You must be Samantha."

"Please, call me Sam."

She stepped out from behind the desk and walked toward me. Her brunette hair was pulled back into a neat ponytail. She wore crisp slacks and a gorgeous red blouse partially covered by a black knitted cardigan. The heels of her leather boots clicked with every step, the sound echoing throughout the room.

"Are any other guests here?" I asked,

Sam shook her head. "We've been fairly busy since it's gotten warmer, but I thought it'd be best to close up shop for a few days while you're here."

"Good call," I agreed. Keeping a business of this kind open while under investigation was a sure way to start rumors and scare off future guests. Then what she'd said clicked. "Wait, you said you've been busy lately. So business must be good then, right?"

"Absolutely." She tilted her head slightly. "Why do you ask?"

"Well, yesterday Mike told me that business had been slow."

Her brows knitted together, matching my confusion. She glanced up the staircase near the desk. Her mouth opened like she was about to say something, then closed again. When she looked back at me, she plastered on a forced smile.

"Let me show you to your room."

Sam helped carry my bags as I followed her upstairs. Halfway down the dimly lit hall, she stopped and nodded toward a door.

"Here you are." She opened it and motioned for me to enter first.

The room had clearly been renovated over the years. The wooden floor and off-white wallpaper peeling at the edges seemed to be the only original features. Although the furniture was newer, the antique theme remained, carrying the faint, nostalgic scent of polished wood—lemon-scented, just like grandma's house on cleaning day.

Along one wall was a queen-sized bed, featuring a dark wooden headboard with an intricate pattern engraved in the center. A fluffy white comforter was spread across it, making it look almost as inviting as mine at home. Matching wooden nightstands stood on either side, each with a fancy lamp that had built-in outlets.

Opposite the bed sat a dresser with a small flat-screen television perched on top. A mini fridge stood beside it, below a shelf that held a microwave and a Keurig. In the far corner was a desk and rolling chair that was sure to leave my body aching if I sat in it for longer than five minutes.

"This looks great!" I exclaimed as I stepped further inside. I set my luggage down at the foot of the bed.

"Dad had the rooms remodeled before reopening," Sam explained.

She set the duffle bag she'd carried next to my things. I expected her to leave right away, but instead, she lingered awkwardly, wringing her hands together and chewing on her bottom lip.

"Are you ready to share more details?" I asked gently. She stayed silent as her eyes darted around the room.

"There's no rush, but the sooner you tell me everything, the sooner I can help."

"I know," she whispered. Eyeing me curiously, she added, "Aside from my dad lying about business being slow, what else did he say?"

"Nothing really," I admitted with a shrug. "He kept rambling about some girl, but he wouldn't tell me who she was. Then we got disconnected."

Sam's eyes widened as all color drained from her face. It wasn't an *oh-my-goodness* look. It was more like an *I-might-know-something-about-this-but-can't-say-it* kind of vibe.

"Why don't we talk about this later?" I offered.

She nodded. "I'll leave you to get settled."

"Sam," I called after her. She paused, looking back at me. "It'll be okay. I promise."

To this day, I still don't know what made me feel confident enough to say those words. In this line of work, we avoid making promises we can't keep—so basically, none at all. The outcome is always as unknown as whatever we're investigating. Promising it would be okay was a risky game.

A hopeful smile spread across her face. Then she turned and left, closing the door gently behind her.

I was feeling drowsy after the long drive. The Starbucks I'd grabbed earlier was not working its usual magic. Knowing sleep wasn't an option, I went into the private bathroom to splash some cold water on my face.

After drying off with one of the neatly folded hand towels, I stared at myself in the mirror, my hazel eyes meeting my own gaze, bright and alert despite my exhaustion. My chest-length blond hair was windswept from driving with the windows down most of the trip. My ivory complexion seemed to glow under the bathroom light, and thankfully, there weren't any dark circles forming beneath my eyes.

The feeling of watchful eyes crept over me again as I unpacked. Suddenly, a loud tapping came from the window behind me. I whipped my head up, heart beating rapidly. *What the hell? I'm on the second floor!* I inched toward the window and peeked around the curtain, half-expecting someone to jump out and yell, "Boo!"

"Phew!" I sighed with relief. It was just a lone tree branch hitting against the glass in the breeze.

To be on the safe side, I dug through my bags until I found my EMF meter (electromagnetic field meter). I turned it on and a single green light came to life. Moving around the room, I scanned for any abnormalities. A movement in the hallway caught my attention, and I headed toward the door.

Suddenly, the EMF meter lit up like a Christmas tree, and the door swung open—revealing a shadowy figure looming in the doorway.

CHAPTER FOUR

A sharp gasp burst from me, my heart hammering in my chest. Then a man stepped quietly from the shadows and into the light. He was middle-aged but handsome nonetheless, with freshly trimmed dark hair that was held firmly in place with enough gel to make Ross Geller proud. His black slacks and matching blazer made him look more like the CEO of a big-shot company than the owner of an old bed-and-breakfast.

I switched off the EMF and slipped it into my back pocket. "You must be Mike."

"Yes," he replied with a stiff smile as he held out his hand. "Ava, is it?"

"Yes, sir." I grinned and shook his hand firmly, then instinctively pulled back. It was so cold it could have belonged to a corpse rather than a living person.

"It's nice to meet you," he said with a short nod. "I trust you're settling in well?"

"I am. Thank you."

We stood there awkwardly for a minute before Mike broke the silence. "This is quite an old building. Are you familiar with its history?"

Shaking my head, I said, "No, sir. Care to educate me?"

He nodded. I dropped onto the edge of the bed and looked up at him, giving him my full, undivided attention.

"My grandpa—Sam's great-grandpa—was ambitious. He bought this old house and turned it into a bed-and-breakfast back in 1949, when he was just twenty-one. It ran for several years before he decided to shut it down. After he passed, my father inherited it.

"He tried reopening it in the early eighties, but it wasn't as successful. Eventually he passed it along to my older sister. She had a business degree, so the family was hopeful it would do well when she reopened it in 1999. It lasted a few years, then she shut it down and passed it to me, saying it was too stressful to run on her own."

"What made you decide to give it a shot after so many failed attempts?" I asked.

"Well, it took me a while to make the decision," Mike admitted. "But I knew it would make my grandpa happy to see the place he'd worked so hard on up and running again."

I smiled up at him. "That's very sweet of you to take him into consideration. Most people would've given up on it."

"I never give up." He smirked.

His determination was admirable. "I'm sure having Sam around makes it easier too."

"It sure does."

"So what made your grandpa shut it down the first time?" I asked curiously.

Mike's smile faltered. He glanced behind him, as if making sure no one was around to hear what he was about to say. In a low, cautious voice he said, "There was a freak accident. In a small town like this, word gets around fast. Over time, it became an urban legend of sorts and scared people away."

"What kind of freak accident?"

His jaw clenched and he broke eye contact. "I'm sorry. I don't know the details."

More lies. But instead of calling him out like I wanted to, I said, "If you're worried about someone overhearing, you can tell me later."

"No." He shook his head and gave a short, nervous laugh. "It's not that."

"Then what is it?"

He met my gaze again, his voice tight and low, "She doesn't want me to talk about it."

A shiver ran through me, sending goosebumps crawling up my arms.

"Who's this girl you keep talking about?" I hoped he would finally answer the question that I'd spent the last several hours thinking about. But Mike just stood there. Fear and sadness mixed in his eyes as he stared at me— almost like he was begging me to help, though I didn't know why or how.

Finally he blinked a few times and cleared his throat. "I have to return to work. Please, excuse me."

"Of course," I replied with a tight nod.

"I hope you enjoy your stay, Ava." He stepped into the hall and shut the door behind him.

I remained seated on the edge of the bed, wracking my brain for answers.

Was Mike talking about Sam? No. I knew that for sure. I would've sensed something wrong about her immediately. Besides, she was just as scared as Mike when discussing anything related to… whatever was going on. And *she* had reached out to *me* for help. There was no way the "she" Mike referred to was Sam.

I stood up from the bed and pulled my EMF meter from my pocket. Flipping it on, I walked over to the door—the same place it had gone wild before.

This time, nothing happened.

My breath caught in my throat as the terrifying truth hit me.

The thing that made it spike before… was Mike.

CHAPTER FIVE

Well, that definitely wasn't reassuring. I set the EMF meter on the nightstand and dug out my notebook. Settling into the desk chair, I wrote down everything that had just happened, hoping it would make more sense on paper.

Afterward, I made a list of possible reasons the meter lit up when Mike was near. I didn't see any devices on him that could've interfered with the signal, and we were not standing anywhere near other electronics.

Maybe there was some faulty wiring in the walls. I mean, the place is well over seventy years old after all.

Or maybe there were some metal clasps—magnetic, maybe—on his clothing, though his business attire didn't seem the type for that.

I even considered the possibility of the meter malfunctioning. But even that didn't seem right considering it was working perfectly fine just a few days ago on another case.

Perhaps Mike really is possessed. No way. Aside from him talking nonsense on the phone the night before, he seemed too *normal*. And the way he kept looking around like someone was eavesdropping on us, it was like he was afraid of an external presence—not struggling with an internal one.

Possession was no longer on the table. I blew out a lungful of air I didn't realize I'd been holding. God that was a huge relief. But what else could be the cause?

Then it clicked. An attachment—a spirit clinging to him, watching and listening to everything. If the spirit had been near him when he was here, it would've definitely set off the meter.

But the question was: who or what was attached to him?

I wrote my conclusion down in the notes, then headed downstairs to find Sam. She was behind the desk again, focusing hard on her work. The bottom step creaked angrily under my weight, and startled Sam. A tiny squeak escaped her. I pressed my lips together in an attempt to hold back my laughter. When she realized it was just me, she rested a hand on her chest as if she could physically slow her heart back down to normal.

"Ava! You about scared me to death."

"Sorry." I gave her an apologetic half-smile. "I just came down here to explore for a bit. Do you mind?"

"Actually, I was getting ready to ask if you'd like to grab a bite to eat with me," Sam said.

As if on cue, my stomach growled. I hadn't consumed anything but Starbucks coffee that morning. "That sounds like a great idea. I'm starving!"

"Let me put this stuff in my office first." Sam nodded toward the pile of papers on the desk.

While she put her work away, I ran up to my room to grab the blue cinch bag I carried everywhere in place of a purse. I shoved my notebook and pen inside, hoping to get more information from Sam once we were away from The Foster House.

As I started to leave, a strange feeling crept over me, like something was off. I did a quick once-over of the room. Nothing looked out of the ordinary. Then my eyes landed on the nightstand.

"What the…" I muttered. My EMF meter was no longer there.

Thinking I might've set it down somewhere else and forgot—proof of my Dory brain at work—I quickly searched the room. Nothing. Sam was probably waiting for me by now, so I made a mental note to look later. Then I left, making sure I closed the door behind me.

I'm positive I left it on the nightstand…

Sam waited by the door with her purse and keys in hand. "Do you want to ride with me?"

"Sure," I replied.

We walked outside and climbed into her little royal blue Ford Fiesta. As we drove into town, I soaked in the calm, homey feel of the small-town life. It was a nice break from the paranormal tension awaiting our return.

"There's a little café here with the best coffee and cheesecake. Want to go there?" Sam asked.

"Yes, please!" I said enthusiastically.

She pulled up beside a small brick building and parked. Inside, the aroma of freshly brewed coffee and baked goods engulfed me. After ordering our food and drinks, we took a seat outside at one of the round bistro tables. Sam was not lying—their coffee and cheesecake were incredible.

Once I swallowed the last bite of my triple-chocolate cheesecake, I asked, "Are you ready to talk about… you know…?" Sam took a sip of her coffee and nodded. I took out my handy-dandy notebook and prepared to take notes. "You mentioned shadows and objects moving"—I paused, recalling the EMF meter vanishing—"what else have you noticed?"

She lifted a shoulder in a half-shrug. "Doors opening and closing by themselves."

"Do you ever get the feeling someone is watching you?"

"All the time." She tilted her head, eyeing me knowingly. "You've felt it too, haven't you?"

"From the moment I arrived," I admitted.

Sam leaned across the table and lowered her voice. "Maybe it's my imagination, but I swear I've seen something moving in the woods. But by the time I step outside to get a closer look, it's gone."

"Like an animal?" I offered. Come on, the place was surrounded by woods. Animals roaming wasn't exactly unusual.

She shook her head. "No. It's human."

"Human?" My brows shot up. Sam nodded slowly and took another sip of her coffee. What would a person be doing out there on their property?

While a draft could cause the illusion of doors opening and closing on their own (please, it's an old building), it did not explain objects being moved around and human-shaped shadows lurking around. And while a person could technically do those things, only Sam and Mike lived there—and neither seemed like the prankster type. Besides, the EMF was triggered by something definitely not human.

"So why do you think your dad is possessed?" I asked, continuing our little Q&A session. Even though I had already determined he wasn't, her insight could still be useful.

Her gaze dropped to the table as she reminisced. "My mom passed away when I was five, so it's been just us most of my life. He's always been the person I looked up to the most—a sweet, funny, outgoing man who worked hard but always made time for his family. The kind of dad every kid dreams of having."

"And now that's changed?" I pressed gently.

Her brown eyes lifted to meet mine and she slowly moved her head up and down. "Not long after we reopened The Foster House, I went out of town for a weekend. When I came back, he was a completely different person and has been ever since."

"How so?"

"He stays in his room all the time, leaving me to do the work alone. He doesn't socialize with the guests; hell, he barely even talks to me. And when he does talk, it's like someone else is controlling his words—draining him of all emotion. Like he's been turned into a robot."

Or a dead person's puppet. "Did the other stuff start happening before or after he changed?"

A crease formed on Sam's forehead. "I'm not sure. I only noticed them afterward. Maybe because I was keeping an eye out for anything unusual that might explain his sudden change."

I nodded as I jotted her answer down. "After you left my room earlier, Mike came to talk to me."

Sam's brows flew up into her hairline. "Seriously? What did he say?"

"He told me the history of The Foster House." I purposely left the part where he rambled nonsense and set the EMF meter off the charts.

"How much of the history did he tell you?"

"Just the basics—previous owners, years it operated, and how he reopened it in hopes of making your great-grandpa proud," I listed.

"Did he tell you *why* it was shut down in the first place?"

I shrugged. "Yeah, something about a freak accident that started an urban legend. Apparently that was enough to scare people off."

"Freak accident?" Sam huffed, shaking her head in disbelief. Then her eyes bore into me. "Try cold-blooded murder."

"Murder?" I acted more surprised than I felt. Hell, most hauntings are the result of a spirit meeting a sudden, traumatic death. "What happened?"

"Rumor has it that in the fifties, a man brought his fiancée to The Foster House for a weekend. Her body was found a few days later in the woods around it. Dude was a sick freak—raped and killed her."

Whether the story was true or not, my heart ached for the poor woman, "Did they ever arrest him?"

"No. They never found him. It's like he vanished off the face of the earth."

"Interesting," I murmured.

Confident I'd gotten everything I needed for now, I put my notebook away and finished off my coffee. Then we headed back to the bed-and-breakfast.

Once we were back in Creepy Town, Sam returned to her paperwork and I went upstairs. Halfway to my room, I came to a quick stop. Even from down the hall, I could see the door was cracked open. I knew damn well I had closed it.

Cautiously, I approached and peered inside.

"Hello?" I called into the seemingly empty room. When no response came, I stepped in fully. I tossed my bag onto the bed and glanced around the room. No signs of an intruder.

Then I saw it.

Sitting on the nightstand, right where I'd left it, was my EMF meter.

"Real funny, Ghostie," I said.

After confirming the device was still intact and functioning, I placed it back on the nightstand. Then I went over to the desk, glancing back a couple of times to make sure the meter didn't sprout legs and take off again.

I sat in the desk chair and tried to get comfortable, but to no avail. "Next time, I'm bringing my own chair," I grumbled.

I opened my laptop and started researching. I already knew the basics about The Foster House—now it was time to dig deeper. Opening a new webpage, I searched for information about the murdered woman.

Much to my surprise, I kept coming up empty-handed. The few articles I did find were on urban legend websites—each one telling a different version of the story, and none of them giving any names to point me on a path. Getting any real information was going to be a challenge.

As I was typing another phrase into Google, the screen went black.

"Dammit," I muttered under my breath. I grabbed my charger and plugged it in. While it powered up, I went downstairs. Sam was perched on a stool behind the desk "Hey, is there a library nearby?"

"There's one in town, but it's closed for the evening. Is something wrong?"

"The internet isn't giving me much to work with," I said. "A local library might have better—and more accurate—resources."

"Maybe I could help?"

Smiling at her kind offer, I said, "I'd appreciate that, but maybe this is a sign I should call it a day."

Sam laughed. "I probably should too."

I waited for her to close up shop, then we went upstairs together.

"This is my room," she said, pointing to the door diagonally across from mine. She made a shooing motion at me. "Now go get some rest. You deserve it."

"If anything happens, come get me. I wouldn't want to miss the party," I joked, giving her a playful wink.

The corners of her mouth tilted up in a small grin. "Don't worry. I'll be sure to wake you." Then she slipped inside her room and shut the door.

I took one step into my room and froze. A soft glow came from my laptop—the one that had been dead as a doornail minutes ago. I moved toward the desk, my pulse quickening with anticipation. When the screen finally came into focus, my chest tightened. An old newspaper article filled the screen, the bold headline reading: *The Murder of Valerie Evans.*

CHAPTER SIX

My eyes remained glued to the screen as I lowered myself into the desk chair. Just below the headline, an old black-and-white photo of a happy couple stared back at me. The caption read: *Warren Williams and Valerie Evans at Riverwood High School Prom (1957).*

The young woman wore a white cocktail dress, her long, dark hair pulled back from her face, showing off laughing eyes and gorgeous smile. She was wrapped up in the arms of a dark-haired man in a suit and bow tie as they danced the night away

But the beautiful moment soon turned into a nightmare as I read the article.

In 1958, Valerie Evans and her fiancé, Warren Williams, had come to The Foster House for a weekend getaway, despite it being illegal for unmarried couples to stay together. Warren's mother stated it was no surprise that he had found a way around the law, calling him a rebel.

The next morning, the couple was late checking out of the master suite. When an employee went to check on them, the room was vacant. Staff assumed the pair had slipped out unnoticed.

When Valerie failed to return home, her family reported her missing and a search began. Her body was found a week later in the woods bordering The Foster House. Authorities ruled it a case of rape and murder.

Leonard Foster, the owner of the bed-and-breakfast, was questioned about why he allowed an unmarried couple to stay on the property. He claimed he had no knowledge of their marital status.

Friends and family described the couple as being madly in love, saying the news came as a shock to everyone who knew them.. Warren was listed as the prime suspect, but his whereabouts remained unknown.

"Oh my goodness," I breathed.

Goosebumps rippled over my skin as a shiver ran through me.

The story pointed directly to Valerie being the entity haunting the place. No wonder the atmosphere pulsed with darkness and restless energy. I still had many unanswered questions, but at least now I had an idea of what—or rather, *who*—I was up against.

I fished my cell phone out of my pocket and opened the camera, snapping a few photos of the article for quick reference later. After bookmarking the webpage, I shut the lid of my laptop and stood up. Since paranormal activity had already been happening in my room, I decided to set up a camcorder to capture any further occurrences—maybe I could even catch a glimpse of the entity herself.

It didn't take long to get one of the camcorders—equipped with infrared night vision, of course—set up in a corner of the room and hit record. In the morning, I planned to do a quick run-through of the footage to see if anything abnormal had happened during the night.

Too exhausted for anything else, I slipped into my pajamas and settled into bed. The warmth and comfort of the blankets enclosing me allowed me to easily drift off into dreamland.

* * * *

Knock! Knock! Knock!

The frantic rapping on my door jolted me awake. I sat upright, fumbling for my phone to check the time. A little after midnight. *Who could possibly be here to pester me at this hour?*

"Come in." My voice was rough from sleep. Okay, inviting an unknown visitor inside while dealing with the paranormal was probably not the best decision of my life. But the sleepy fog hadn't lifted, so I wasn't thinking clearly.

The door creaked open and Sam stepped into the room. It was too dark to make out her expression, but I could sense something was wrong.

"What happened?" I asked, scrambling out of bed.

"Don't you hear it?" she whispered.

"Hear what?" I whispered back.

She held a finger to her lips, signaling for me to hush. Then the sound drifted to me—a mixture of a moan and a grunt, almost animalistic, which made sense being surrounded by the wilderness.

Then I realized it was coming from *inside* the building.

"What the hell is that?" I asked, my face scrunching in confusion.

"I don't know," Sam said. "But it always happens around this time."

"Every night?" I asked. She shook her head. "Have you noticed a pattern?"

She thought for a moment, then said, "No. It just happens randomly."

"How long does it last?"

"No more than a couple of minutes."

I turned my head from side to side, trying to figure out the source of the sound. "Where's it coming from?"

"I'm not sure." She gave me a sheepish look, lifting one shoulder. "I've always been too scared to find out."

I dashed across the room, snatched the EMF meter off the nightstand, and shoved my phone into my pajama pocket before heading for the door.

Sam grabbed my arm. "Where are you going?"

"To find out what's making that noise," I said, grinning like The Doctor when something exciting is about to happen. "Care to join me?"

"Well, I sure as hell am not letting you have all the fun," she said, giving me a once-over.

Together, we roamed the second floor, following the strange sound. We turned a corner into a short hallway with three doors: one on either side and the third at the very end. By now, the volume had increased drastically, and the sound of someone talking joined in. I paused, listening intently. It was a man, but I couldn't make out what he was saying.

I gestured for Sam to stay while I tiptoed down the hall.

I narrowed the sound down to the door at the very end. Moving quickly, I approached it and raised the EMF meter. It went full-blown disco mode, alerting me that something paranormal was near.

Let's see what's behind door number one.

My hand barely grazed the doorknob when something suddenly gripped my forearm, making me jump.

"Don't go in there," Sam warned, her voice trembling.

I turned to look at her. Her eyes were fixed on the door, wide with fear, and her breathing had become uneven.

"Why not?" I asked.

"That's my dad's room."

My hand dropped instantly, as if the knob had been set on fire. A chill swept through me as I recalled the EMF meter going crazy when Mike came to my room.

There were now two things I was absolutely certain of: one, Mike was being followed by something—perhaps Valerie—and two, I had absolutely no idea what to do about it.

"Come with me," I said, wrapping my arm around Sam and ushering her back to my room.

Once there, she collapsed onto the edge of the bed. I paced in front of her, my thoughts racing. I wasn't entirely sure what was going on, but I knew it would not be solved with a simple cleansing or kindly asking the entity to leave the family alone. An attachment involving a woman who died a horrific death was going to require a little more effort.

Which meant I needed backup.

I glanced at Sam, who was still shaking and clearly trying to keep herself together. She would later prove useful in the case, but right now I needed someone with actual paranormal investigation experience.

My stomach clenched, warning me against my next move. But I didn't have any other options.

"You can stay in here tonight," I told Sam. "Just hang tight. I'll be right back."

I rushed into the bathroom and shut the door firmly behind me. It wasn't until I pulled my phone from my pocket that I realized my hands were trembling. Encountering creepy—and sometimes downright terrifying—things wasn't new to me (hello, it comes with the job). But I'll admit, whatever was going here had me a little on edge. Taking a few deep breaths to calm myself, I hit the call button.

A groggy but concerned voice answered. "Ava? What's wrong?"

"Austin, I need you."

CHAPTER SEVEN

"What's going on?" Austin suddenly sounded wide awake, as if my cry for help had yanked him straight into reality.

"I-I'm not sure," I stammered. The superpower he usually had—the ability to calm me down with just the sound of his voice—seemed to be malfunctioning.

Because it's not his voice you need… it's him.

"Do you know what you're up against?"

"A vengeful spirit… I think." I hurried on before he could question it. "A woman was murdered here, and I believe it's her spirit raising hell, but that's all I know."

"Dammit, Ava," he muttered, frustration lacing his words. Then his tone softened. "What have you done so far?"

"Not a whole lot except take a bunch of notes." God, was I the worst paranormal investigator or what?

"That's a good start."

I inhaled deeply, filling my lungs, then let everything spill out in one breath. "This isn't as clean-cut as I hoped it would be. It goes way beyond what I can handle on my own. Not to mention I don't have much equipment—and what I do have is so outdated…"

"Ava—" Austin started.

But I continued to ramble, my words pouring out faster. "You're so much better at this than I am. You have all the equipment and more experience. You were right before—I shouldn't have taken this case alone. You should've come with me. I need you, Austin."

"Ava," he repeated, louder this time, and followed by a small chuckle. "Calm down. You are smart, talented, and brave. You're doing everything you can with what limited knowledge and resources you have. I'm proud of you."

My heart squeezed at his unexpected praise. Swallowing the lump in my throat, I asked, "What do I do now?"

"You wait for me."

"It's the middle of the night." *Excellent point, Sherlock.*

Austin lived closer to the Oklahoma-Arkansas border than I did, but he'd still have a solid three-hour drive to get here. And I seriously doubted he'd gotten much sleep yet.

"I know," he said simply. "But you need me."

A slow smile spread across my face, and my chest fluttered softly. Just like that, the panic and lingering fear melted away, replaced by the comfort of knowing he would be here soon.

"Thank you." I said it so quietly I wasn't sure he'd even heard me.

"Hang in there," Austin said. "I'll see you soon."

When the call ended, I returned to the bedroom. Sam hadn't moved an inch, but at least she had stopped shaking. I plopped on the bed beside her.

"Are you okay?" I asked gently.

"I think so." Her tone was not very convincing. Then she blew out a long breath. "It's just so weird, you know? I've heard that sound so many times, but it never scared me like this."

"Maybe that's because you didn't know where it was coming from," I said.

Her head tilted to the side. "What do you mean?"

"Well, before it was just a strange noise." I said slowly, carefully choosing my words so I didn't frighten her more than she already was. "Now you know it's coming from your dad's room, and you're worried about him."

"I suppose you're right."

Sam rose from the bed and crossed the room to the closet, grabbing some blankets and a pillow from the top shelf. She nodded toward the bathroom. "So… who were you talking to in there?"

"Oh, that was my friend, Austin."

"You mean the really hot guy in some of your videos?" Her voice had a little too much excitement for my liking.

"Yeah. Him." My cheeks became hot, and I was thankful Sam was too busy arranging the blankets and pillow on the floor in the corner to notice. "He's coming to help out. I hope that's okay."

"Fine by me." She flashed me a mischievous grin as she settled onto the floor. "So he's just a friend, huh?"

I shrugged, doing my best to sound casual. "Of course. What else would he be?"

"Oh, I don't know… a *boyfriend* maybe?" Sam said, giving me a look that clearly said I wasn't fooling anyone. I narrowed my eyes at her, and she threw her hands up in mock surrender. "I mean, who else would drive to another state in the middle of the night just to help a *friend*?"

"Whatever." I scoffed, rolling my eyes at her. "Let's get some sleep."

I crawled under the blankets for the second time that night, my mind still in overdrive. Worry gnawed at me over what was happening in Mike's room, and Sam's flopping and muttered grumbles as she tried to get comfortable on the floor didn't help. But eventually, exhaustion won the battle, and I drifted off into nothingness.

* * * *

The sudden vibration of my phone near my head pulled me back to consciousness. I propped myself up on one arm and answered the call.

"Hey," I whispered, trying not to disturb Sam, who was finally sleeping peacefully.

"Hey," Austin's deep, steady voice came through on the other end. "The door is locked. Can you let me in?"

"I'll be right down."

I slipped quietly out of bed and headed out of the room, toward the stairs. On my way, I passed the hallway leading to Mike's room and paused, peering into the dark corridor. Silence. Whatever had been there hours before was gone.

Reminding myself that someone was waiting for me, I hurried down the stairs and into the lobby.

I turned the lock on the knob, slid the chain free, and threw the door open. The sky was deepening to a rich blue as the sun began its ascent. Austin stood, a duffle bag slung over his shoulder. At his feet rested a hard-sided case holding his most advanced, expensive equipment for intense investigations, and a backpack with the smaller, more practical tools used for everyday paranormal work.

He wore dark jeans and a black *Ghostbusters* T-shirt. The porch light reflected off his dirty-blond hair, which fell in tousled waves that nearly covered his ocean blue eyes.

"Come here," he said, holding his arms wide as he smiled down at me.

I didn't hesitate. Stepping into his warm embrace, I inhaled his familiar scent of cedarwood and fresh sage. For the first time since arriving, I felt safe—protected.

A twig snapped near the trees, and both of us whipped our heads toward the sound. Austin squinted, trying to see what was lurking in the darkness. "We should go inside."

"Good idea," I agreed hastily.

I reached for the backpack at his feet just as he picked up the hard case. Once inside, I led the way upstairs to my room. Sam was pacing back and forth anxiously.

"Thank God you're okay!" she breathed, a rush of relief washing over her.

"Sorry," I said, surprised by her worry. "The door was locked, so Austin called me to let him in."

"Oh. Hi," she said, as if just noticing him standing beside me. "I'm Sam. It's nice to meet you."

"Likewise," Austin replied with a nod.

After placing his belongings on the floor next to mine, he began unpacking. Sam and I sat on the bed, legs dangling off the foot, watching him. There was something so… attractive about the way he studied each item, his face so hard and serious and—

Suddenly, Sam inhaled sharply as she sat up straighter. I glanced at her, puzzled by the reaction. "Wait. You said the door was locked?" she said.

"Yes." I dragged out the word.

"We never lock that door."

I looked at her as if she'd just spoken a foreign language. *They never lock the door?* Coming from the city, I couldn't fathom why anyone would leave their home unlocked.

"Dad was going to get keys made so each guest could come and go freely, but he hasn't gotten around to it yet," she explained. "Crime isn't really an issue here, and our personal belongings are locked in our rooms."

Austin stopped what he was doing and faced us, arms crossed over his chest. "If you didn't lock it… then who did?"

"I'm guessing the entity we're after," I said.

Sam frowned. "What does that mean?"

Austin met my gaze and gave a subtle nod, confirming my unspoken suspicions. Valerie had known he was coming.

His jaw tightened, his expression darkening. When he spoke, his voice was flat and steady.

"It means I'm not wanted here."

CHAPTER EIGHT

A surge of panic shot through me as I realized Austin being here could make everything go wrong—and potentially put him in danger. Now it made sense why my gut had been screaming not to bring him.

I opened my mouth to suggest that maybe he just should leave his equipment with me and go home, but Sam spoke first. "Why wouldn't it want you here?"

"Any number of reasons, really," Austin replied, shrugging as if it were nothing. "But I'm sure we'll find out soon enough."

He flashed me a confident grin, tinged with a hint of cockiness. I forced a smile in return, but inside, my mind whispered, *Just hope it isn't too late when we do…*

Sam announced she was heading out for an early start, then slipped quietly from the room, leaving Austin and me alone. The door clicked shut behind her, and he turned to face me.

"What do you know about this entity?"

"Not much," I admitted, rising from the bed to grab my laptop and notebook from the desk. "Here are the notes I've taken."

I handed him the notebook, and he sat on the edge of the bed to study it. Taking a seat next to him, I opened my laptop and pulled up the article about Valerie's death. It didn't take him long to review everything.

"It sounds like Valerie is the culprit. She definitely has the motive," he said."

"That's what I thought, too."

Austin shifted to face me, his captivating eyes holding mine. "What was happening when you called me?"

"Sam woke me up because she heard a noise."

"And?" he prompted impatiently. "What kind of noise?"

My forehead creased as I searched for the right words. "Almost like the groaning sound someone makes when they're aggravated—but more beast-like."

"Was that the first time she'd heard it?"

"No. Apparently it happens around the same time of night, but not every night. She hasn't noticed any pattern for when it occurs, and it's possible she sleeps through it sometimes."

Austin nodded slowly, showing he was following along, then gestured for me to continue.

"We followed the sound to another room. I heard a man talking as we got closer, but couldn't make out the words."

"Did you go inside?"

"I was going to, but Sam wouldn't let me—it's her dad's room."

Austin's head jerked back in surprise. "Wow. Okay… did you have the EMF on you?"

I nodded. "It went crazy just like when Mike came in here yesterday. I think Valerie is following him."

"Out of everyone who lives and stays here, why would she choose to follow *him*?" He rubbed his chin thoughtfully as he stared past me.

I chewed the inside of my cheek, hesitant to ask the next question—and afraid of the answer. "You don't think he's possessed after all, do you?"

His eyes flicked back to mine. Touching my arm gently, he said, "This isn't that kind of case. I promise."

If Austin said it wasn't possession, then it was true. His reassurance eased the lingering uncertainty I'd been feeling.

"Now what?"

"We need to set up some hidden cameras in Mike's room to see what's going on in there," he said.

"Sam might be able to help with that."

"That would be great," he said, nodding.

Knowing I would not be able to fall asleep again, I grabbed a set of clean clothes from my duffle bag and headed to the bathroom to get ready for the day. Before going in, I glanced back at Austin, still sitting on the bed and flipping through the notebook.

"Shouldn't you get some sleep?" I asked.

"I'll be all right."

"You've been up most of the night."

He met my eyes and smirked. "Wouldn't be the first time."

In our line of work, staying up for hours on end was normal. But that didn't stop me from worrying about his lack of sleep. Eventually, he'd crash—and what if it happened when I needed him the most?

Get a grip, Ava. He's a big boy. He knows what he's doing.

By the time I changed and freshened up, Austin was propped against the headboard. He stared at his laptop like he was trying to crack the code to the universe. I sat beside him and saw he'd pulled up the article about Valerie.

"Is this the only thing you've found about her?" he asked.

"So far. I was hoping to visit the local library today to see what else I could dig up."

Austin cocked his head toward the camcorder in the corner. "Did you capture anything interesting overnight?"

"You mean besides Sam and me having a mild freakout session?" I raised a brow, then shrugged. "I haven't had the chance to look yet."

"Want me to check it for you?"

"Go for it."

I dug through my equipment bag until I found the cable that connected the camcorder to the laptop. Then I grabbed the device off the tripod.

"I should go tell Sam about our plan to get into Mike's room," I said, passing the cable and camera to him. "Why don't you come down too? There's plenty of space to sit and watch nearly twelve hours of absolutely nothing."

"Yeah, sure."

He scooped up his laptop and followed me downstairs.

"We need to get into your dad's room," I told Sam, cutting straight to the chase as we reached the desk.

She tore her eyes away from the pile of paperwork she'd been buried in and looked at Austin and me. "Huh? Why?"

I leaned over the desk, lowering my voice to a whisper. "We need to set up some hidden cameras."

"When?"

"The sooner, the better," I replied.

She chewed her bottom lip and glanced upstairs. "I don't know if that's possible..."

"Make it possible."

Austin's voice took on that authoritative tone I knew all too well. He meant business. Sam seemed to pick up on it immediately, nodding in understanding—this task was important and not up for debate.

"Okay. Maybe I can talk him into going somewhere. How long do you need?"

"An hour, tops," Austin said.

"I'll see what I can do," she said. "Just give me a few minutes. I'll let you know the plan soon."

We thanked her and stepped into the little common area. Austin dropped onto the red antique sofa in front of the fireplace and immediately got to work reviewing the camera footage. I, on the other hand, couldn't sit still. I wandered around the downstairs area, waiting for Sam to give us an update.

I had just completed a lap around the perimeter when a movement outside caught my attention. My eyes flicked to Austin, who was so focused on his task he probably wouldn't have noticed if the building were burning down around him.

As I stepped closer to the window by the fireplace, a shadowy figure glided along the treeline beside the building.

"Austin." I said quietly, as if the being could hear me through the brick wall.

No response.

I watched the figure as it drifted deeper into the forest.

"Austin," I hissed loudly, snapping my fingers at him while keeping my gaze glued to the creature.

"What?"

I waved him over. He came to stand beside me, and I pointed to the human-like figure that had gone still.

"Do you see that dark shadow over there?"

He followed my finger and squinted to see clearly. Suddenly, the figure's head snapped toward us, as if it had been listening the entire time. Its eyes seemed to glow faintly in the dim light. Then, just as quickly as it appeared, it scurried off into the forest.

"Holy shit," Austin breathed, stepping back from the window. "Was that… a person?"

"I think so."

"Didn't Sam say she'd seen a shadow person out there before?" he asked.

I nodded. "Do you think it—"

I was cut off by someone clearing their throat behind us.

Austin and I spun around to see Mike standing practically on top of us. *Is he wearing the same clothes as yesterday?*

"Good morning, Mike," I said with a friendly smile.

"Good morning. I trust you slept well?" His voice was polite, but he didn't return my smile like he had the day before. That was not a good sign.

"Of course," I said. When his gaze flicked to Austin, I added quickly, "This is my friend, Austin."

"Nice to meet you, sir," Austin said.

"You as well," Mike replied with a short nod.

Silence stretched as Mike stared Austin down, studying him closely. Was it my imagination, or did he seem uneasy about Austin being here?

"So, Mike," I began casually, breaking the tension and bringing his attention back to me. "Did you hear anything unusual last night?"

His eyes narrowed. "What do you mean?"

"Well, Sam and I thought we heard some weird groaning noise in the middle of the night," I explained. When he remained silent, I shrugged and continued. "I'm sure it was nothing."

"I don't recall hearing anything." His gaze shifted to the window behind me. "We get quite a few wild animals out there. Perhaps that's what you heard."

I pressed my lips firmly together to stop myself from calling him out on yet another lie. Instead, I nodded. "That must've been it."

Mike's attention slowly returned to us. "I'll leave you two be while I check on my daughter. I hope you have a wonderful day."

He turned and crossed the room. As I watched him go, my stomach tightened.

How long had he been standing behind us? Long enough to see the shadow? Long enough to hear us whispering our suspicions?

Whatever the answer was, Mike knew more than he was letting on—and secrets like his had a way of getting people hurt.

CHAPTER NINE

"Well… that was weird," Austin mumbled, but I was too lost in my own thoughts to respond.

He lightly touched my arm before returning to the sofa. I remained rooted in place, watching Sam and Mike talk among themselves. They were speaking too low for me to catch anything.

After what felt like forever, Mike nodded at something his daughter said. Then he turned and headed up the stairs. Once he was out of sight, Sam waved me over.

"I asked him to go pick up some groceries," she whispered, as if worried someone might overhear us.

"How long will that take?"

"The store isn't far, but it should give you a full hour at least," she replied. "Get ready to do what you need to. I'll let you know when he's gone."

"Okay. Thanks."

I quickly filled Austin in on the plan, then we gathered our things before returning to our room. Austin rummaged through his backpack, double-checking that everything we needed was there. As I shoved my EMF meter into my jeans pocket, my phone dinged with a message from Sam.

"The coast is clear," I told Austin, slipping my phone into the other pocket.

"Let's roll," he replied, slinging the backpack over his shoulder.

We hurried to Mike's room. I tried to turn the doorknob, but it was locked.

"Hang on." Austin set the backpack on the floor and pulled a small lock-picking kit from the front compartment. It didn't take him long to get the door open; it was definitely not his first rodeo.

The door swung inward and a blast of cold air slammed into us.

"What the hell?" Austin muttered.

"It's freezing in here!" I exclaimed, wrapping my arms around myself. "How is that possible? It's the end of May!"

"The better question is," he said, stepping inside, "how does Mike live in here?"

Cold spots are common with hauntings, but we definitely weren't prepared for Mike's bedroom to feel like a secret portal to Antarctica. Okay, maybe that was a bit dramatic. Still, it had to be around forty degrees, which was way too cold for someone who only packed T-shirts (unfortunately, that someone was me).

Thick curtains covered the window, blocking out most of the sunlight that might've warmed the room a bit. I ran my hand along the wall until I found the light switch and flipped it on.

While Austin got to work installing the hidden cameras, I began searching the room. The first thing I noticed was how outdated everything looked, as if the space had been preserved exactly as it originally was. But why renovate all the other rooms and leave this one untouched?

A large black-and-white portrait of a man hung on the wall in a tarnished gold frame. It stood out—not just because it was the only decoration, but because it wasn't even centered. That bothered me… and made me curious.

I carefully lifted the frame off the nail and set it on the floor, leaning it against the wall.

Behind it was a dent in the wall not much bigger than my fist.

"I wonder what happened here," I said loud enough for Austin to hear.

"Looks like someone lost their temper," he joked from across the room. Then his tone shifted. "Hey, can you hand me the precision screwdriver kit in my bag?"

"Sure." I went to the backpack and retrieved the small plastic container that housed the tiny screwdrivers, then brought it over to him. "So, did you find anything interesting on the footage from last night?" I asked, watching him work on the little screws holding the camera together.

His blue eyes flicked to mine, and a mischievous grin tugged at his lips. "You mean besides Sam thinking I could be your boyfriend?"

"Sam has issues," I stated, keeping my voice casual even though my face was turning a very unattractive shade of red.

Austin laughed under his breath and shook his head, amused, before returning his focus to the miniature camera. When he finished with the kit, I put it back in his backpack and resumed my investigation.

Using my cellphone, I snapped a photo of the dent in the wall before carefully rehanging the portrait. As I scanned the room again, another oddity caught my attention—an old red floral rug. Or rather, the *placement* of it. One corner was tucked under the nightstand, and it ran the full length of the bed.

After finding something of interest behind the portrait, curiosity had me locked in. I knelt down to get a closer look at the tattered rug. Nothing about it seemed unusual, but my instincts told me to dig deeper.

I rolled it up, starting from the foot of the bed, exposing the hardwood floor underneath.

Scratch marks covered the area. They were quite small and appeared in no particular pattern, making it difficult to determine the exact cause.

"Look at this," I called over to Austin.

He crossed the room and crouched beside me. His brow furrowed as he examined the floor.

"What do you think those are from?" I asked.

"No clue," he replied, scratching his chin. "But we're going to find out."

He went to his backpack and pulled out a small UV light. After switching off all the lights in the room, he returned to my side and clicked it on, bathing the space in a purple glow.

We studied the marks closely. Bright green specks reflected back at us from inside some of the scratches.

"Is that glass?" I asked, leaning in for a closer look.

"It's the right color for it," Austin said as he stood. "It would also explain the scratches. It doesn't take much to gouge wood like this. Walking on shards of glass in a sturdy pair of boots would do the trick."

I began rolling the rug back into place but noticed Austin hadn't moved. He stared intently at the floor, head tilted slightly, as if he were analyzing a lab sample.

"What's wrong?" I asked.

He nodded toward the floor. "Do you see those dark spots?"

Under the UV light, faint black streaks and splatters surrounded the scratch marks. I was surprised I hadn't noticed them sooner.

"Yeah," I said slowly. "What are those?"

"Only a liquid could've left stains like that," he explained.

"Blood?"

Austin nodded.

I took the UV light from him and scanned the surrounding floor. Nothing unusual appeared.

"It's only under the rug," I said.

"That area probably hasn't been clean or seen the light of day in years," he replied. Then he glanced around the room and his expression shifted. "This is the master suite."

I blinked at him, confusion written all over my face.

"The article said Valerie stayed in the master suite the night she died," he continued.

"But her body was found in the woods," I pointed out. "And the article made it seem like there was nothing out of the ordinary when the room was inspected."

"The police could only document what they saw," he said. "If they'd seen this, it would've been in the report."

"Then someone must've cleaned up the worst of it and kept the police out of the room," I said, following his line of thought. "But her fiancé was nowhere to be found. So who could've done it?"

Austin lifted a brow as the pieces slid into place. "Sounds like old man Foster died with a little secret."

CHAPTER TEN

So this is where Valerie was murdered. Spirits often have strong ties to the place they died, especially when the death is traumatic. It made sense for her to frequent the master suite—and her continued presence explained the abnormally cold room.

"If she comes here because she's attached to the room, not to Mike, then why don't we just get him to switch rooms?" I asked, hopeful that all our problems had just been solved. But then Austin opened his mouth and ruined that.

"I wish it were that simple."

"Why isn't it?" I asked.

"You heard a man's voice in here last night, then Mike denied anything abnormal going on," he said. "He's hiding something, Ava. If it were as simple as a ghost dropping by for a slumber party, he wouldn't be lying—especially to us."

My shoulders slumped forward and I blew out a lungful of air. I knew he was right. Unfortunately, we still had a long way to go.

Austin turned the lights back on and finished setting up the last camera. I was photographing the scratch marks when my phone chimed with a text message.

Mike was turning into the driveway. I quickly rolled the rug back into place while Austin crammed everything into his backpack. Then we hightailed it out of the room, making sure to lock the door behind us. Otherwise, Mike would definitely notice that something had happened in his room while he was gone.

"Do you think we should tell Sam what we discovered in there?" I asked as we arrived back at our room.

"That's your call," Austin said.

Part of me felt obligated to keep her updated on the investigation. But the other part knew she was already shaken and didn't want to push her over the edge. I mean, how exactly do you tell someone their dad is bunking with the ghost of the girl whose murder case their family helped cover up?

While I was weighing the options, Austin held his hand out, palm up.

"Give me your phone."

I glanced at his hand, then back up at him, confused. "Why?"

"I'm going to connect it to the cameras like mine."

"Oh," I replied simply, handing him my phone.

While he installed the app and worked on getting it connected, I went downstairs. Sam and Mike were carrying bags of groceries into the dining room. Sam spotted me lingering near the stairs and came over.

"Did you have enough time?" she asked quietly, so her dad wouldn't overhear.

I gave a quick nod. "Come to our room when you're done here."

About five minutes later, Sam arrived. Austin was sitting at the desk, searching for something on his laptop. I was sprawled out on my stomach on the bed, scrolling through the photos I'd taken in Mike's room, and trying to figure out how to explain it all to Sam in the least terrifying way possible."

"Did everything look normal in there?" she asked, dropping onto the bed beside me.

"Well… not exactly."

"What do you mean?" Her voice thickened with concern.

I passed her my phone with the images pulled up. She scrolled through them carefully as I explained what Austin and I had seen under the UV light—the tiny shards of glass embedded in the wood and the faint traces of blood.

"What happened in there?" she asked, handing the phone back.

"It's where Valerie Evans died," I said.

"Who?"

"The girl from that urban legend." I pushed myself up into a sitting position and shrugged. "Turns out the legend has some truth to it."

"So now your dad has an obsessive roommate who's made herself right at home," Austin added cheerfully from across the room.

"What!" Sam screeched.

I threw Austin a *way-to-go* glare, which he happily ignored. Then I turned back to Sam, racking my brain for words that wouldn't terrify her further.

"Mike isn't possessed, like you originally thought," I assured her. "But for some reason, Valerie has chosen to attach herself to him, influencing his words and actions. We don't know why yet, but we'll figure it out."

"She's the one making those weird sounds at night," Sam said.

It wasn't a question, but I answered her anyway. "Most likely. We'll keep an eye on the cameras to see exactly what's going on."

Tears welled in Sam's eyes, her voice cracking. "Will my dad be okay?"

I had already promised her the day before that everything would be fine—but would it be? Not wanting to make any more promises I might not be able to keep, I said, "We'll do everything we can to keep him safe."

Sam sighed heavily, then said, "Is there anything I can do to help?"

"You're welcome to help us with research," Austin offered.

"Does the library in town have a microfilm or archives section?" I asked.

She knitted her brows thoughtfully. "I don't remember, but you'd probably have better luck at one of the larger libraries in Little Rock."

Since it was still early in the day, Austin and I agreed to make a trip into the city. Sam, knowing the area better, drove.

The library was busier than I expected for a weekday morning. We found an empty table along one wall near a computer station. Though our goal was to dig through the old archives, we decided to exhaust most of our internet searching first. Austin and I sat next to each other at the table and opened our laptops. Sam chose a computer nearby and began her own search.

A few minutes had passed—though it felt like hours—when Austin scooted his chair closer to me, angling his laptop so I could see the screen. He casually draped his arm over the back of my chair.

"Look at this," he said.

The earthy scent wafting off him made my pulse spike, and I struggled to focus on the police report he was showing me.

According to the police, Valerie's naked corpse was found in the woods by The Foster House, covered in patches of dried blood. She had several bruises and lacerations, and some of her fingernails were missing. A few yards away lay a shredded, blood-soaked blanket, tangled in a pile of brush. Investigators concluded that she had apparently tried to escape the brush but perished during her attempt to seek help.

"So she didn't die in the room," I said after finishing the report.

"Actually, she wasn't anywhere near dead yet," Austin replied, clicking over to another tab that displayed the autopsy report.

It stated that Valerie had died from a severe brain hemorrhage caused by trauma to the head. According to the medical examiner, the severity of the hemorrhage would normally have taken twelve to twenty-four hours to be fatal, but they believe the exertion she used while trying to escape the brush caused her death to occur much faster.

"Oh my God," I breathed. "How can people be so cruel and heartless?"

"I don't know," Austin said softly.

He printed copies of the two reports while I returned to my task. Now that we knew what happened to Valerie, it was time to figure out what her plans were with Mike.

I spent another hour rewording search phrases and scrolling through page after page of results. Finally, I came across a website that proved to be very useful. I got Sam's attention and waved her over.

"Didn't you say the place closed because of Valerie's death?" I asked.

"That's how the story goes," she replied with a half-hearted shrug.

I pointed to the article on the screen. "Well, according to this, it didn't close until a couple of years later—after two more deaths occurred."

"Let me see that," Austin said, leaning over to get a closer look. After reading it, he eyed Sam questioningly. "Why did it shut down the other times?"

"I was told it was because of lack of business," she said.

"Do you remember the exact years it was open when your grandpa and aunt owned it?" I asked.

Sam bobbed her head. I slid her my notebook so she could write the years down. Once she finished, I noted the names of the two people who had died after Valerie, along with their death dates. Then I closed my laptop and gathered my belongings.

"Where are you going?" Austin asked curiously.

"To check the archives," I said, looking between him and Sam. "Either of you want to help?"

"I will," Sam offered.

"I'll keep searching online a bit longer," Austin said.

Sam and I tracked down a librarian who showed us where the old newspaper microfilms were kept. We grabbed a basket and filled it with reels from the years her family operated The Foster House. Lack of business no longer seemed like a believable explanation. I needed to know the *real* cause.

When the basket was full, Sam and I headed into a small room that branched off the archives section and held a handful of unoccupied microfilm readers. We each picked one and got to work. I was so absorbed in the task that I nearly had a heart attack when Austin suddenly appeared in the chair beside me.

"Find anything good?" he asked.

"No," I grumbled.

"Well, I did," he said proudly, laying a neat stack of freshly printed papers in front of me.

I thumbed through them and was baffled by what I saw. Over the years, there had been several reports of people around the country who had gone to Little Rock—mostly for business—and returned home completely changed. Some were deemed clinically insane and received psychiatric treatment. Others weren't so lucky and ended up taking their own lives. The interesting part? They were all men. The names of the victims—dead or alive—were listed at the bottom of the page.

"Okay, but this doesn't mention The Foster House," I pointed out. "What makes you think it's related to this case?"

"Hey, it's more than you've come up with," he said defensively. Then he flashed a boyish grin and nudged me with his elbow. "But maybe it's a lead on a future case."

I shoved him playfully and turned back to the microfilm I'd been working on. Austin still seemed convinced the papers meant something. As he read through them again, he highlighted certain details.

"Guys, I think I found something," Sam said, gesturing toward her reader.

I leaned in to look. Big, bold letters at the top of the screen read: *Horror House Claims Its Sixth Victim*. I was instantly hooked and read on.

Early this morning, the body of Kevin Hess from Springfield, Illinois, was found at The Foster House. Hess' family stated he had gone to Arkansas for his high school reunion and never returned home. His death appears to be a case of foul play, but there are no known suspects at this time. Guests and employees were questioned and claimed they didn't see or hear anything abnormal throughout the night.

This marks the sixth person to meet a tragic end at the small-town bed-and-breakfast just minutes outside the city limits since it opened in 1949. Authorities believe all six deaths may be connected, but there are currently no leads.

The names of each victim—including Valerie Evans, the only female—were listed at the end of the article. I snatched the papers from Austin's hand; he had highlighted the names of the deceased victims. I compared them to the ones on the microfilm.

"They're the same people," I said, mildly surprised. Passing the papers back to Austin, I added, "I guess that does relate to our case after all."

"Told you so." He smirked. Before I could respond, he looked past me at Sam. "What's the date on that?"

She scrolled to the top and read, "August of 2010."

"The year your aunt closed it," I said.

"Yeah. She told us she just couldn't handle the stress of running the place on her own anymore."

"I guess now we know why she was stressed," I muttered before turning to Austin. "Can you find the police and autopsy reports on Kevin Hess?"

"I'm on it," he replied.

Sam and I waited impatiently as he opened his laptop and began the search. Thankfully, it didn't take long for him to find what I needed.

Clearing his throat, Austin gave a brief summary. "Kevin was found mostly naked, with his clothes ripped to shreds and multiple lacerations covering his body. They initially thought he was mauled by a wild animal."

"An animal?" Sam asked, furrowing her brow. "But the other article said he died at The Foster House."

Austin clicked to another report, raising one shoulder in a half-shrug. "Technically, he did. They found his body in the woods."

"Just like Valerie," I added.

He nodded and continued reading. "During the autopsy, they found bruises around his neck made by human hands. The cause of death was strangulation and blood loss."

I pointed to another name on the list of victims. "Check the reports on this one."

He quickly found the reports and skimmed them. "It's identical to the other one."

"I bet they're all like that," I said.

"And there's no doubt Valerie is behind them all," Austin added.

"How did she manage to lure them into the woods, though?" Sam asked, tilting her head curiously

"Spirits can possess some very powerful abilities," I explained.

Austin glanced at her. "Is your grandpa or great-grandpa still alive? They might know something that could help us."

Sam shook her head sadly. "They both died before I was born."

"I'm sorry." His words were gentle, empathetic even, but I could see the curiosity in his eyes. "How did they die?"

Somehow I knew what she was about to say, but still something inside me went cold as she spoke the word out loud.

"Suicide."

CHAPTER ELEVEN

Austin and I exchanged a quick glance. His slight nod told me he'd reached the same conclusion as I had. Sam's eyes flicked between us as suspicion sharpened her features. She knew we were holding something back.

"What is it?" she asked hesitantly, like she wanted to know but was afraid to ask.

Austin handed her the papers about the men who'd gone insane, pointing out the specific paragraph that discussed those who had committed suicide. Sam bit her bottom lip, holding back her emotions as she read. When she finished, she handed the papers back to Austin and stared down into her lap.

"That's what happened to my grandpa and great-grandpa, isn't it?" It hurt my heart to hear her voice tremble with so much sadness.

I laid a comforting hand on her arm. "We don't know that for sure, but it's possible."

She raised her head, tears rolling down her cheeks. "And that's what will happen to my dad too."

"No it won't," I assured her quickly, though deep inside I had my doubts.

"We'll stop it before then," Austin said, sounding far more confident than me.

Silence fell over the room as we each got lost in our own thoughts, absorbing everything we'd just discovered.

Finally, I broke the silence. "I think we've done enough for today."

While Sam and Austin loaded the reels back into the basket, I jotted down notes on the article she'd found. Then the three of us returned to the main area of the library.

"Hang on, I want to search one more thing before we go," Austin said.

He went over to the table we'd been at earlier and pulled out his laptop. In the meantime, Sam and I returned the microfilms to their proper places. By the time we finished, Austin was grabbing a stack of papers from the printer.

"Now we can go," he said as we approached him.

"What'd you find?" I asked.

He handed the pile to me, and I flipped through it. They were obituaries of all the men who had died because of The Foster House—whether at the cold, dead hands of a vengeful spirit or by their own.

"Maybe we can make a connection between them," Austin suggested. "Fgure out why Valerie would prey on them specifically."

"Good idea," I agreed.

A cocky grin spread across his face. "Yeah, well, I do get those occasionally."

Back at The Foster House, Sam stayed downstairs, leaving Austin and me to sort through the stack of obituaries in peace. He sat cross-legged on the bed and spread the pages out between us. As we read through each one, I wrote down anything that may be comparable among them—age, gender, occupation. Then I compared the dates and times they died.

The minutes turned into an hour, and still nothing was falling into place. A soft knock came at the door and Sam poked her head inside.

"I thought I'd drop in to see if you've come up with anything yet," she said.

"No," I grumbled. "The only thing these men had in common is that they were… you know… men."

Austin let out a mock sigh of relief as he wiped invisible sweat from his forehead. "Oh thank God. For a minute there, I thought I was in danger." Even though he was trying to play it cool, his eyes told a different story: he was scared.

"Maybe you should go home," I told him. "You could help with the research from there, without putting yourself in danger here. I can handle everything else on my own."

He scoffed. "Please. It's gonna take a lot more than being the prey of a dead chick to scare me off."

I rolled my eyes. "You're crazy."

"You have no idea," he said with that adorably cocky grin and a mischievous twinkle in his eyes.

Sam, now camped out at the desk, snorted and tried to cover it with the fakest cough I'd ever heard. I shot her a look, which she answered with a smug little smirk. Austin was too busy frowning at the obituaries, totally oblivious to what was going on around him.

"I don't get it," he muttered.

"Get what?" I asked.

"I'm sure there have been way more men here over the years who didn't have anything happen to them. So what was her motive for *these* guys?" He waved a hand at the papers.

I shrugged. "I guess we still have a lot to figure out."

"What if you found the guy who killed her?" Sam suggested. "Would that do any good?"

"He's probably dead already for all we know," Austin said. "Even if he's alive and justice is served, it may not be enough to put her spirit to rest and stop her from doing whatever the hell she's been doing."

Sam's face became a giant question mark, so I simplified it for her. "Basically, we need to get all the facts to make an informed decision on the right approach."

"What would happen if you made the wrong choice?" she asked.

"Then the wrong things could happen to the wrong people." I spoke slowly, letting my words sink in. Her face dropped as she understood what I was implying.

"Well, I'm beat," Austin said, cutting through the tension in the room. "Mind if I crash for a bit?"

"I need to get back to work anyway," Sam said, rising from the chair. "It's tough running this place on my own. On the bright side, having you two here is giving me time to catch up on paperwork."

Then she slipped out of the room. Austin picked up his duffle bag and went into the bathroom. I wandered over to the window near the bed and looked out over the surrounding forest. It felt nice to finally have a moment alone. The sun had lowered behind the trees, casting long shadows that seemed to dance in the breeze.

I sighed as I rested my head against the window. *What is going on here?* I went over everything in my head for the hundredth time, trying to make sense of what we'd discovered and what was still missing. Suddenly, one of the shadows that had blended into the trees moved. I jumped back from the window as a small squeak escaped me.

Then the remaining bit of my sanity yeeted itself into oblivion and I made the decision to go out there and approach the lurker on my own. Without giving myself time to chicken out, I scooped up my camcorder and EMF meter and rushed to the door. I ran straight into Austin as he was emerging from the bathroom.

"Whoa! Where's the fire?" He chuckled, grabbing my arm to keep me from falling on my butt.

"Sorry, I, uh…" My voice trailed off as I took in the sight.

Austin was shirtless. Actually shirtless. All he had on were red plaid pajama pants, and for a second, my brain forgot how to function. Three years of knowing him and I'd never seen this much skin. It wasn't that he was hiding anything; we just never ended up in a situation where going without a shirt was necessary. No swimming, no beach vacations, and he always crashed in an old T-shirt. But now? There was nothing between me and the sight of a very real and very toned set of abs. Not a crazy bodybuilder six-pack, just a soft, subtle outline that made my stomach do cartwheels.

"Ava?" he asked, instantly snapping my attention back up to his face.

The corners of his mouth twitched upward as he fought to hide his grin. He definitely noticed me gawking at him like an idiot. Great. Absolutely fantastic. I swallowed hard, pulled myself together, and somehow managed to form words again.

"I was just going to capture some footage downstairs. You know, see if I can pick anything up on camera." It wasn't a total lie; outside was technically downstairs.

"All right. I'll be here if you need me."

I remained rooted in place, hesitant to leave him alone. But he needed sleep, and I had a job to do.

"Hey." The softness in his voice showed that he had sensed my inner turmoil. "Go do what you need to. I'll be okay."

"Okay," I said reluctantly.

As I headed out of the room, I glanced back at Austin. He gave me a sleepy grin and a knowing wink before climbing into bed. Suddenly aware that I'd already wasted too much time, I bolted downstairs, desperately hoping the lurker was still... well, lurking.

"Sam," I said breathlessly as I reached the lobby. "Can you come outside with me?"

"Why? What's wrong?" She was equally confused and concerned by my urgency.

All in one breath I described what I had seen from the window that morning and again just a minute ago.

I told her I wanted to check it out and that I suspected it was Valerie.

"It'd be great to have someone with me for safety," I finished.

"Yeah, I'll go," she agreed without thinking twice about what she was getting herself into. Then she nodded toward upstairs. "Are you sure it's safe to leave Austin alone?"

"No. But he needs sleep," I said. "Can you man the camcorder for me while we're out there?"

"Sure. No problem."

I gave her a quick rundown on how to work the camera, then we headed outside. We walked toward the woods swiftly, but quietly. As we approached the tree line, a rustling came from up ahead.

"Are you sure this is a good idea?" Sam whispered nervously.

"We'll be fine," I said, dodging her actual question.

Slowly, we inched our way deeper into the woods. The lack of rain recently left the ground dry and crispy. Our footsteps echoed loudly in the quiet forest.

Quiet forest? I paused to listen. Nothing. No birds chirping their happy little songs. No squirrels parkouring from tree to tree. Just silence.

I glanced at Sam. She held the camera steady and aimed toward me, but her eyes darted around as if visually documenting the nearest escape route. We continued our trek, our path becoming darker as the canopy of trees overhead thickened, blocking out most of the sunlight. Eventually, we came to a small clearing. Here I could see open skies above and what light remained from the setting sun flooded the clearing.

Then the rustling came again; much closer this time. I motioned for Sam to stay at the edge of the clearing while I stepped into the center of it.

I inhaled deeply and, upon exhaling, called out to the dead. "Valerie!"

Nothing happened.

"Valerie!" I shouted again. "If you're here, show yourself."

More rustling came and my head whipped in the direction of it. There was a flash of movement among the trees a few yards ahead. I stared hard and damn near peed myself when half of a woman's face suddenly peeked out from behind a thick tree trunk.

My hand flew up to my chest as I gasped. When my breathing settled back to normal, I spoke softly to the woman. "I'm not going to hurt you. I just want to talk."

From behind the safety of the tree, her dead, sunken eyes stared at me; never blinking. Thirty seconds passed, then a minute. Finally, she emerged from the shadows and into the light. Heartache washed over me as I took in the awful sight.

Her naked, pale gray body looked relatively normal—for a dead girl. Her dark, nappy hair fell past her shoulders, barely covering her breasts. As my eyes trailed down, I took note of several cuts and bruises that never had the chance to heal. Patches of dry blood and decayed flesh covered her from head to toe.

Sam gasped loudly from behind me. I turned to see her staring at Valerie, eyes bulging as her trembling hands struggled to hold on to the camera.

"She won't hurt us," I assured her. Then I turned back to Valerie, meeting her dead, glassy stare. "I've been learning a lot about you, and I want to help."

She continued to give me that blank look. I needed to get some answers out of her, but I didn't know what to say without scaring her off—or worse, making her angry.

"Are you here because you want revenge for what happened to you?" I asked. She nodded slowly. "I know Warren did this to you. Is he still alive?"

A mixture of pain and betrayal flashed across her face at the mention of her fiancé-turned-murderer. But all she did was shrug in response.

"Then why can't you get your revenge on him and leave my family alone?" Sam demanded to know. Valerie and I both flinched at her sudden outburst.

"She can't leave," I replied, keeping my eyes locked on Valerie. "If she could, she would've by now. But her spirit is trapped here." Not knowing how much time I had before she vanished, I hurried on with my next question. "Where can I find information about Warren?"

Without warning, Valerie stepped around me and headed directly toward Sam.

"I don't know anything, I swear!" Sam screeched as she stumbled backward, eyes darting around frantically.

Shaking her head, Valerie continued past Sam, following the path we'd taken to get there. Sam and I exchanged a confused look, then followed her. She stopped just before the tree line. Then she lifted one arm and pointed straight ahead. For the first time I noticed dried blood was caked where her fingernails once were. Wrinkling my nose in disgust, I tore my gaze away from her hand and looked where she was pointing.

The side of The Foster House was barely visible through the thin layer of trees. I scanned the building like I was playing a game of *I Spy*. Finally, I saw it, and my blood ran cold.

Standing behind one of the second floor windows, staring directly at us, was Mike.

CHAPTER TWELVE

I turned back to Valerie to ask for confirmation, but she was gone. I looked around the area, thinking she'd just stepped back into the shadows out of Mike's line of vision, but she was nowhere to be found.

"Where'd she go?" Sam asked, eyes searching the area frantically, as if she expected Valerie to pop up again like some horror movie jump scare.

"I don't know," I said. "But we should go back inside."

Sam passed me the camcorder, and we headed back inside. She went over to the fireplace and let herself drop onto the sofa.

"That poor girl!" she cried.

"I know. It's terrible," I agreed as I took a seat beside her.

She looked off into the distance, chewing her bottom lip. "Do you think my dad actually knows about Warren?"

"He might not know where he lives, but I believe he might know *something* that could be useful." I frowned and added, "He doesn't seem too open to answering questions though."

"So what now?"

"We need to track down Warren. But before we do that, I still want to figure out what all the victims had in common." I rested my chin on my hand and furrowed my brow. "We're missing something. I just know it."

Sam gave me a knowing smile. "Translation: you need to make sure it's safe for a certain someone to be here."

"Is it a crime to want to protect my best friend?" I tried to sound defensive, but the smile in my voice was a dead giveaway.

Sam cocked an eyebrow at me. In an attempt to steer the topic back on track and make some progress, a thought occurred to me. "Hey, do you keep old guest records?"

Sam nodded. "There are several boxes of them in the office."

"How far back do they go?"

"To the beginning of time," she said. "I've been meaning to destroy them because we have no use for them, but I haven't gotten around to it yet."

"Can we look through them?" I asked hopefully.

"Sure. I'll bring them into the dining room." She got to her feet and walked off. As she passed the staircase, she looked over her shoulder and grinned. "In the meantime, you should probably check on Prince Charming."

I rolled my eyes and laughed. "Shut up."

I needed to grab the list of victims I'd left in the room anyway. Hell, why not make sure Austin is still breathing while I'm in there? I went upstairs and slowly opened the door. Austin was sleeping peacefully on top of the blankets, right where I'd left him. Trying not to disturb him, I snuck over to the nightstand and scooped up the papers before quickly retreating from the room.

Downstairs, Sam was sitting at a table in the dining room with several old cardboard file boxes neatly stacked on the floor. I sat in the chair across from her and took the lid off the first box. It was packed full of paper guest records, neatly organized in manilla file folders. Each file was labeled with a month and a year.

"This is going to take forever," Sam groaned as she stared down at the boxes.

"We'll narrow it down by only searching for the records that match the dates of these deaths." I turned the paper with the victims' names so she could see it.

"Good idea."

"Well… maybe we should try to find the records for the ones who went inside too," I said. "But we don't need all of them."

Sam agreed to that plan, which narrowed our search down from several years' worth of records to just five days—one for each victim, excluding Valerie. We each grabbed a few random files too, hoping to find records for some of the living ones.

We sifted through hundreds of papers in silence for a while. As we found one we needed, we'd lay it off to the side and put a checkmark next to the name on the list.

"So, what's the deal with you and Austin?" Sam asked like we were best friends in high school.

I plastered an innocent look on my face and played dumb. "What do you mean?"

"Please." She scoffed. "It's obvious you two have a thing for each other." When I didn't respond she added, "Well? Am I wrong?"

"Yes… well, no," I said, not really sure how to answer.

She lifted a brow at me. I blew out a long breath and confessed the truth. "Look, I've had feelings for him since the day we met, but I don't think his feelings are mutual. And I'm afraid of telling him how I feel, making things awkward, and then losing him as a friend."

"Oh, trust me. The feelings are totally mutual," Sam replied with a smirk. She leaned back in the chair and waved a hand toward the stairs. "Go on. Tell him how you feel. You can thank me later."

I snorted a laugh and shook my head in amusement.

When she spoke again, all of her playfulness had vanished. "I gotta ask, what made you agree to come all the way out here to help us?"

"After talking to Mike on the phone, I thought you might be right about him being possessed," I said. "I couldn't let another family suffer from that."

She tilted her head curiously. "Another family? You've dealt with possessions before?"

I hesitated, afraid to share my story with her… or with anyone for that matter. The only person who knew about it was Austin and the police. Of course, Austin was the only one who knew the *truth*. But something inside me was saying I could trust Sam to listen and not judge.

Inhaling deeply, I began to share the biggest mistake of my life. "Two years ago, I was called to investigate some paranormal activity at a home in Edmond, Oklahoma that a family had just moved into. Almost immediately I discovered a demon in the house—it had already possessed the dad by the time I got there."

I shifted uncomfortably in the chair and continued. "I hadn't dealt with a demon before and was scared. So I left. The mom followed me out to my car, begging me to help them, but I couldn't—I didn't know how. I told her to go back inside, grab her two kids, and get the hell out of there." I hung my head, ashamed to admit the rest. My voice cracked as the words spilled out. "Then I got in my car and drove away."

"Why didn't you call Austin like you did this time?" Sam's tone was surprisingly soft—not harsh and condescending like I partially expected it to be.

"He was on another case in Boston at the time."

"Did the family get out safely?" she asked inquisitively.

Tears burned my eyes and I swallowed the lump in my throat. "No. About a week later I saw on the news that everyone in the house had been found dead. Police called it a murder-suicide, with the dad being the killer. But I knew the truth—the demon made him do it." I shook my head in disbelief, still unable to forgive myself. "The mom was three months pregnant. Five innocent lives were taken because I was a coward. So when I thought

Mike was possessed, I saw it as an opportunity to right my wrongs."

"Ava, you did the best you could. And you probably saved yourself in the process." Sam reached over to place a comforting hand on my arm. Her brown eyes met my hazel ones as she continued. "Just like you're doing the best you can now. Remember that."

I hadn't realized I was crying until a single teardrop fell on the paper in front of me. Wiping my face with the neck of my T-shirt, I gave her a small, appreciative smile and got back to work.

Once I had pulled myself together again, I asked, "Did you and Mike always live in this little town?"

Sam shook her head. "I was born in Arizona. After my mom died in a car accident when I was five, we moved to Little Rock—his hometown. We just moved in here a few months ago when the place was officially reopened."

"I'm sorry about your mom," I said gently.

"Sometimes I wonder what life would be like now if she were here." The corners of her mouth lifted ever so slightly as she added, "But I think Dad has done a pretty bang up job on his own."

I smiled at her. "He sure has."

For the next several minutes we focused solely on our task, saving the idle chitchat for later. Finally, we had accumulated all the records I felt were necessary. Sam put the boxes away in the office while I arranged the papers in date order.

"Austin and I will be staying up to monitor the camera overnight," I told Sam once we were back in the lobby. "You're welcome to join us."

"Sounds like we're going to need a lot of snacks and energy drinks," she replied, which I took as a yes. "We can run to the store in town."

My eyes drifted upstairs. "I don't know. Stepping outside was one thing, but completely leaving him behind…" I shivered as I imagined all the terrible things that could happen to Austin in the short time we'd be gone.

"I feel the same way with my dad," Sam admitted quietly. "I'm afraid of what I might come back to sometimes."

We gave each other sympathetic looks, not really knowing what to say to make the other feel better in the moment.

"How about I go get the stuff and you can stay here to protect lover boy and my dad?" she offered.

I nodded in agreement. Sam grabbed her purse and keys from behind the desk and left. I watched from the window to make sure she was safe until the little blue Fiesta disappeared from sight. Then I glanced at the grandfather clock. It wasn't as late as I expected — only a little after seven in the evening — yet I was starting to feel drowsiness settling in. *God, this is going to be a long night.*

Upstairs, I opened the door to my room slowly and peered inside. Austin was still passed out on the bed. Tiptoeing over to the desk, I sat down in the poor excuse for a chair. I opened my laptop, plugged the camcorder into it, and waited a couple of minutes for the footage to load. My mouse hovered over the play button, getting ready to click it, when the bed suddenly creaked behind me. The chair made an awful squeak as I spun around to face the bed.

"Good morning, sunshine," I greeted Austin cheerfully.

He pulled himself upright and ran a hand through his messy blond hair, yawning. "Did I miss anything?"

"Not really. I had a little talk with Valerie," I said casually, as if it were a typical, everyday occurrence. He sat up straighter and started to speak, but another big yawn overtook him. "Oh, and Sam and I found the guest records that match the five men who died here, and some of the ones who went insane."

"Tell me you're joking." His voice was low and strained, yet curiosity flickered in his eyes, hungry for more details.

"No." I waved the papers in the air. "They're right here."

He pinched the bridge of his nose, trying to keep a grip on his patience. "Not that. The part about talking to Valerie."

"Right. Yeah. That's not a joke either."

"Is that why you were in such a rush earlier?" he asked, eyeing me suspiciously.

I nodded, beaming proudly. "I caught the whole thing on camera. Come watch."

He leaned back against the headboard, groaning. "I don't want to move."

Lifting my eyes heavenward, I sighed dramatically. I grabbed the laptop and camcorder and took a seat on the bed beside him. He managed to draw up enough energy to move closer to me so we could both see the screen. Then I clicked play.

Once the video ended, I turned to Austin. "Any thoughts, questions, or concerns?"

I had expected him to ask questions about Valerie or Mike. But his one-track mind was focused on someone else… *me*. More specifically, how I handled everything.

"Were you scared?" he asked.

"At first," I admitted. "But once I saw her—saw proof of the horror she'd be through—my fear went away. It's like she was no longer a vengeful spirit. She was just a woman who'd been hurt and needed help."

A hopeful look came across him. "So you don't think we're in any danger here?"

"*I'm* not," I said firmly. "But *you* are."

His eyes, blue as the sea, locked onto mine, and my breath caught in my throat. He leaned in closer until our foreheads were almost touching.

"I'll be fine," he said, his voice low and still gravely from sleep. "I promise."

My mouth opened—probably to blurt out something stupid—just as the door swung open. Austin and I jumped apart guiltily, like we'd been caught doing something we shouldn't. Sam stood in the doorway with bags of goodies dangling at her sides.

"Am I interrupting something?" she asked innocently, the corners of her mouth twitching upward.

"Not at all," I said, a little too quickly to be convincing.

Austin cleared his throat awkwardly as he dragged himself out of bed. He grabbed a fresh change of clothes from his duffle bag and made a beeline for the bathroom without making eye contact with anyone.

"I'm going to take a shower," he announced before as he shut the door firmly behind him.

"Uh, yum," Sam said as she stared after him. "No wonder you're in love with him."

I shot daggers at her—which she ignored—then she began putting the drinks in the fridge. I got up and helped her by organizing the snacks on top of the dresser. There was more than enough to last us for a few days. Hopefully we finished the job long before then though.

"So, did you kiss him?" Sam teased as she gathered the empty bags and shoved them into the trash can.

"No!" I exclaimed.

She put a hand on her hip and wagged a finger at me. "I swear I'm going to hurt you if you don't make a move before all this is over."

When she turned her back to leave the room, I stuck my tongue out at her like a little kid. She came back shortly after, carrying a book and a phone charger. I sat on the bed again while she curled up with her book in the corner.

Eventually, Austin emerged from the bathroom wearing his usual loungewear—gray sweatpants and a Disturbed T-shirt (his favorite band). He crossed the room to his backpack, rummaging through it until he found a tabletop phone tripod. After he attached his phone to it, he placed it on the nightstand and pulled up the live footage of Mike's room.

Mike was facing the window, staring outside just like when I was talking to Valerie. *Has he been there this whole time?*

"Let's take a look at those guest records you found," Austin told me.

I collected the papers from the desk and settled in beside him on the bed, sitting criss-cross applesauce while he propped himself against the headboard. He took the pages from me and studied each one carefully. The seconds turned into minutes as I eagerly waited for him to finish, hoping he'd come up with something—*anything*—that could give us answers.

"Well, well, well," he muttered in amusement as he came to the last record. "Would you look at that."

"What?" Sam and I asked in unison. I looked over to see her walking toward us.

"The master suite," Austin said quietly. Then he looked at me. "They all stayed there."

CHAPTER THIRTEEN

"I guess you have your answer to what they all have in common," Sam said. "Do you have everything you need to make a decision now?"

I wanted to say yes, but the sudden clenching of my gut was telling a different story.

"Partially," I said

She and Austin threw looks of confusion my way, so I continued. "It tells us why they were targeted, but it doesn't answer why some were killed and others weren't. How did some of them get away? And what caused them to go insane afterward? You can't tell me it happened because they encountered a ghost." I turned my palms up in a half-hearted, sarcastic gesture. "Hello. I've seen Valerie. She isn't *that* scary."

"Which means you still don't know how to get rid of the problem," Sam added with a frown.

I gave an encouraging half-smile. "No, but we're getting closer."

Satisfied with my reassurance, she went back to the corner and opened her book. Austin and I started going over all of the information we had collected… *again*. A few minutes later, a loud *thud!* came from across the room.

Sam had fallen asleep and dropped her book. Chuckling, we turned back to the papers scattered on the bed.

Since I wasn't getting anywhere in my own head, I started to share my thought process out loud. "Valerie admitted she's here for revenge. Judging by the information we have so far, it looks like she's trying to reenact her own death in a way by assaulting them and leaving them for dead in the woods."

"But what makes her choose who to kill and who to spare?" Austin asked. After a moment, his face turned from thoughtful to absolutely disgusted. "You don't think she…"

"What?"

He shifted a little to face me. "Well, she was raped. These men were found with their clothes ripped off. What if she's been… you know… propositioning them?"

"That would definitely be enough to drive anyone insane." I shivered, scrunching my face. "But ew! God, I hope that's not it."

"I don't think we'll get any answers out of Mike. So there's only one other way to find out," he said.

"How?" I asked cautiously.

The thought of Austin camped out in the master suite, waiting for Valerie to come work her mojo on him, made bile rise in the back of my throat. Thankfully, that was not the plan he had in mind.

Tapping one of the papers, he said, "We see if any of these guys are still alive to tell the tale."

"Sounds like a plan," I agreed.

I retrieved my laptop, ready to begin yet another round of research. No doubt it would be harder than usual considering we had very little information to go off of. Not to mention the majority of them had the most basic, common names in the world. Seriously, how many Joseph Williams does the world need?

"Stephen 'Steve' Smith," Austin said randomly after a few minutes. To this day, I don't know how he narrowed it down to one person out of the hundreds in existence with the same name.

"Huh?" I asked brilliantly.

He passed me one of the paper records. "He stayed here in 2008."

"Where is he now?"

"In a long-term psychiatric facility in Memphis, Tennessee," he replied.

I pulled up the GPS on my phone. "That's about two hours from here."

"Are you up for a road trip in the morning?" He grinned, holding his fist out to me.

"Always." I smiled back, bumping my fist against his.

Since we had travel plans the next day, we decided to sleep instead of monitoring the cameras all night. I took a steaming-hot shower, letting all of my cares wash down the drain. For the first time in two days, I felt totally relaxed. I didn't realize how long I'd been in there until the water started to become tepid. I slipped into a pair of joggers and an old Lynyrd Skynyrd T-shirt before stepping out into the bedroom.

The lights had been turned off, but the moonlight pouring in through the window offered enough illumination to make it to the bed safely. Austin was watching a video on his phone when I returned to my spot on the bed. A giant yawn escaped me .

"Tired?" he asked, chuckling softly.

Leaning against the headboard I said, "Not at all."

He cleared his throat—his number one sign of nervousness—and said, "So should I sleep here or…"

We'd slept in close quarters before—small motel rooms, tight budgets, and a whole team of paranormal investigators packed in wherever they fit. It kind of came with the territory.

Still, it would be the first time Austin and I shared a bed *alone*.

And I couldn't exactly make the poor guy sleep on the floor. That would be rude.

"Up to you," I said, avoiding eye contact.

"Cool," he replied. The smile in his voice released a kaleidoscope of butterflies in my stomach.

Without another word, I slid under the blankets and turned onto my side, facing the door. Austin went back to watching a video. Sometime later, the bed moving pulled me back into consciousness, but I did not have enough energy to investigate. It took a few seconds to realize it was just Austin getting settled in for the night. As a protective hand rested on my side, I fought to keep my breathing slow and even, hoping he didn't know I was awake. Luckily, I didn't have to fake sleep much longer as exhaustion took over and I succumbed to the darkness once again.

* * * *

The click of a door shutting awakened me. I sat up, rubbing my eyes to clear my vision. The soft moonlight that had filled the room before had been replaced by the blinding sun. I glanced at the corner and saw Sam had already left.

"Good morning, sleepyhead," Austin said, wide awake and ready to go as he exited the bathroom. He wore a pair of dark blue jeans and a short sleeve plaid button-down shirt, left open to reveal a dark gray shirt underneath.

"Morning," I grumbled sleepily.

"Get up," he said, clapping his hands together. "We have a big day ahead."

I hauled myself out of bed and got ready for the day. When I returned to the bedroom, Austin was grinning like an idiot while lightly bouncing from side to side.

I narrowed my eyes in genuine concern. "What's wrong with you?"

"We're going on an adventure!" he shouted enthusiastically.

"You are so weird," I muttered under my breath as I walked past him.

By the time we were ready to leave, the sleepy fog had lifted and I was able to function properly. Austin shoved a handheld voice recorder in his pocket before we headed downstairs.

"Good morning," I greeted Sam as we entered the lobby.

"Likewise," she said. "Did you two sleep well?"

"Are you kidding? I hadn't slept that good in ages," Austin said.

"Imagine that," she said, her tone full of mock surprise. Then she quickly changed the subject, lowering her voice. "I didn't hear anything last night. Did you?"

I shook my head. "But I'll check the camera footage while we're on the road to see if anything happened."

"Wait, what? You're leaving?"

"Only for a few hours," I said.

"One of the survivors is living in a psychiatric facility in Memphis," Austin explained. "We're hoping to get some answers from him."

"I'm presuming you'll want to stay here instead of tagging along," I guessed.

Sam nodded. "Go do what you need to do. I'll call if anything exciting happens here."

On the way to Memphis, I used my phone to check the footage from Mike's room. Nothing out of the ordinary happened all night. It was a relief, but it still left us with no answers on what Mike was experiencing in there.

The remainder of the drive was spent with us being our typical crazy selves. We were having such a blast that, for a moment, I almost forgot why we were on the road to begin with.

But reality smacked me upside the head when Austin steered the Lexus into the parking lot of the facility. We climbed out of the car and crossed the lot to the front entrance. The white, four-story, hospital-like building towered in front of us with *State Institution of Memphis* in gigantic letters on the side. A sidewalk wrapped around the building, with benches and flower beds lining it on either side. Above the automatic glass doors hung a large canopy; giving the place almost a luxurious feel.

Inside, the lobby was comparable to a fancy hotel. A loveseat and two matching upholstered chairs were arranged around a fireplace, creating a cozy sitting area. A forest green runner covered the floor leading from the door to the reception desk. The receptionist looked at us and pasted a totally fake smile on her face.

"Hello," she welcomed us in an overly perky voice. "How may I help you?"

"We're here to visit a man named Stephen Smith," I said, sliding her a scrap piece of paper with his name and address scribbled on it.

"What are your names?" she asked, searching the computer.

"I'm Ava Moore and this is Austin Reed."

She squinted at the screen and said, "I'm sorry. I don't see your names here as approved visitors."

"We're psychology students over at Vanderbilt," Austin lied smoothly. "Our professor was supposed to send over an email regarding this visit as part of a class project."

The receptionist stared hard at him. I held my breath, waiting for her to call him out on his lie and kick us out of the building—ruining our chances of knowing what was really happening at The Foster House.

"Let me check with my supervisor," she said finally. "Excuse me."

As soon as she was out of hearing range, I turned to Austin and whispered harshly, "What the hell are you doing?"

"Just trust me," he mumbled back, his lips barely moving.

When the receptionist returned, she had a paper in her hand. "I apologize for the wait. It seems the email was just sent out this morning, and the note hadn't been put in the system yet."

"No worries," Austin told her with a friendly smile.

"I just need to see some photo ID from both of you."

We handed her our driver's licenses. Luckily, we didn't have to fake that part since a lot of university students are from out of state. She scanned our IDs and handed them back to us, along with some forms to fill out. Then she told us to have a seat in the lobby.

It had only been about ten minutes when a young woman in light blue scrubs called our names and instructed us to follow her. As we stepped through the large wooden double doors, the place suddenly felt, and looked, more like a prison than a place to help the mentally ill feel better about themselves.

She ushered us into a small room with lockers for us to store our belongings in. Since this visit was for a "school project," Austin was granted permission to bring the voice recorder along.

After being patted down to make sure we had nothing on our persons that was illegal or could be used as a weapon, the nurse led us down another hall into a private space that was set up like an interrogation room—complete with a two-way mirror along the back wall.

Austin and I took a seat next to each other at the rectangular table in the center of the room. The nurse told us to sit tight, then left. Austin placed the recorder on the table and pressed the red button. Soon, the door opened and another nurse—a man this time—stepped into the room.

"Here you go, Mr. Smith," he said, directing a disheveled man to the table. "Have a seat right here."

The man wore a white scrub top and matching bottoms, sporting a hospital bracelet on his left wrist. His brown, shaggy hair looked like it hadn't been touched in months. Emptiness filled his hazel eyes, and his face was void of all emotion. He dropped heavily into the seat across from us.

Before leaving, the nurse said, "I'll be watching from the next room. Signal me when you're finished."

"Hi, Steve," Austin said the instant the three of us were alone. "I'm Austin and this is Ava. We're students at Vanderbilt and would like to interview you."

Steve stared down at the table—not moving, not blinking. Great. How were we supposed to get any information out of this guy? I knew we had to stick to our little white lie Austin created to get us in here, but we also had to find a way to get Steve to talk.

I leaned forward slightly, lowering my voice. "We know about The Foster House."

It was enough to capture his attention. His gaze lifted to meet mine. Though his face remained blank, his eyes flickered with surprise and a touch of fear.

"It would help us a lot if you shared your story," Austin said.

Steve looked at him and scowled. "Nobody else believes me. Why would you two be any different?"

Austin shrugged in a way that said *try us*. "You'll find we're a little more open-minded than the others you've talked to. We've had our fair share of"—he paused, carefully choosing his next words—"abnormal encounters, I guess you could say."

Steve studied us, trying to read our expressions, which I hoped relayed the hidden message we couldn't say out loud.

"Students, huh?" he said.

Austin nodded and gave him a wink.

"Well, then. What do you want to know?"

"Everything that made you end up here," I said. *Now we're getting somewhere!*

He exhaled deeply, letting his eyes fall to the table again. Then he began. "I had to attend a last-minute business meeting in the dead of winter in Little Rock. For whatever reason, the boss man booked my room at The Foster House instead of somewhere in the city. Something didn't feel right about the place."

"How so?" I asked.

"It made me feel… uneasy—like I shouldn't be there."

Austin nodded like he had experienced the same thing.

"The woman working that night warned me the thermostat was broken, so I'd have to rely on a space heater to keep the room warm," Steve continued. "It was a useless piece of shit, so I took a hot shower to warm up a bit. When I came out of the bathroom, a woman was sitting on my bed. I don't even know how she got in my room."

"What did she look like?" I questioned. Now that I'd met Valerie personally, I could determine if the woman he encountered was her or not.

Steve gave a small shrug. "She was young—maybe nineteen or twenty, if I had to guess. She had long, dark hair and was absolutely stunning. But she was naked, which was… strange. And she kept staring off into space, like she was high or something.

"When I asked if she was okay, she jumped like I had scared her—like she didn't know I was there. Then things got even weirder. Out of nowhere, she started putting her hands all over me and kissing me." His face scrunched up at the memory. "I told her I had a girlfriend, but she didn't seem to care. She wouldn't take no for an answer, no matter what I said, so I had to use some force to push her away."

"Did she get mad?" Austin asked.

Steve snorted a humorless laugh. "Yeah, I guess you could say that." His eyes narrowed as he shook his head. "She gave me a choice."

I knitted my brows together. "A choice?"

His jaw clenched and anger burned in his eyes. "Yes. Either I had sex with her, or she'd kill me."

Austin and I shared a look, and I knew we were wondering the same thing. *Why would Valerie do that?* Being a victim of sexual abuse, it made more sense for her to force herself up on the person, just as her fiancé did to her. Revenge at its finest. Something was not adding up.

Maybe he's exaggerating his story to make whatever happened next seem…better.

"I thought she was messing around, just saying nonsense like a lot of intoxicated people do," Steve said. "But then… changed."

"Changed?" Austin lifted a brow.

"She turned from this beautiful young woman to a living corpse, just like that," he said, snapping his fingers. "Her body was all beat up. I knew something awful had happened to her. And there was blood… so much blood…" His eyes glistened with unshed tears, and his body had begun to tremble.

"Take your time. We're in no rush," I said gently.

"Then I knew she was serious. My girlfriend was pregnant with our first child. I had to live for both of them. So I… I did it." The dam inside of him finally broke. Tears poured down his cheeks as his shoulders shook with every sob.

"What happened after… you know," Austin said, trying—and failing—to hide his disgust.

"She disappeared."

I was beyond grateful Austin did not ask for further details. Instead, he asked, "How did you end up here?"

"I was having nightmares every night, and I couldn't make love to my girlfriend anymore. Nor could I explain why. She thought I was cheating on her. My mental status and my relationship both going downhill affected my job too, and I became unemployed a month later. My family feared for my safety and forced me to come to this hellhole." His voice dropped so low that I barely heard him mumble, "Sometimes I wish I'd chosen death."

"What did you tell the doctors?" I asked.

"Everything I just told you. But nobody believes me."

I held his gaze and said, "We believe you."

"Is there anything else you'd like to share with us?" Austin asked.

Steve pursed his lips together, shaking his head. Austin turned in his chair to face the two-way mirror and gave the nurse behind it a thumbs-up to signal that we were done.

"Thank you for sharing your story," I told Steve. "It really helps us a lot."

He looked between Austin and me, his eyes boring into ours. "Stop whatever is happening there before more people get hurt."

"We will," I assured him evenly.

The nurse returned to take him away. When they got to the door, Steve looked over his shoulder at us one last time.

"Thank you for believing me," he said quietly before following the nurse out of the room.

The same woman who escorted us to the room came back to lead us out of the building, stopping to get our belongings from the locker along the way.

As Austin and I were walking back to the car, I glanced sideways at him and asked, "How'd you manage to pull off that whole Vanderbilt story?"

"A magician never reveals his secrets," he said, flashing me a mischievous grin and a wink.

I smiled briefly, then asked, "Do you think Steve was telling the truth?"

"It's disturbing, but believable. I mentioned the possibility of Valerie propositioning the men, but this choice"—he put air quotes around the word—"she gives them just doesn't make sense. She was raped *and* killed—I doubt she had a choice in the matter. So why give others one?"

"I was wondering the same thing." I sighed, feeling a little bummed out. "I wish more people knew the things we know. Too many innocent people get thrown into these places just because others are too close-minded to believe anything that doesn't involve science."

"I feel you there," Austin said.

We hopped into his car and hit the road, stopping for some very unhealthy food from that overly greasy place with a big golden M along the way.

"I'm really glad you were willing to join me on this case," I told Austin as our journey neared its end. "Even if your life is hanging in the balance."

"Hey, I'll always be there for you," he said softly.

"What if I'd been farther away? Like in Europe?" I watched his reaction closely, curious to know if his face would say something that his mouth wouldn't.

A quiet, breathy laugh escaped him as a smile tugged at his lips. He shrugged. "Then it would've taken me a little longer to get to you."

"You still would've come?"

"Of course," he said, as if the answer should have been obvious. "No matter where you are, I'll always be there when you need me."

"Really?" I asked in awe.

He looked over at me for half a second, warmth shining in those deep blue eyes as his smile widened.

"Really."

CHAPTER FOURTEEN

The moment Austin and I came through the door of The Foster House, Sam bombarded us with questions. Instead of answering right away, I told her to come upstairs with us. In the privacy of our own room, the three of us sat in a circle on the bed, like we were preparing for a seance. Austin laid the sacrificial voice recorder in the center and hit play.

Once the recording finished, I looked at Sam. All of the color had drained from her face, and I couldn't figure out if she was going to throw up or pass out. But instead, she just sat there, staring down at the recorder like it was a landmine she'd found herself trapped on.

When she finally spoke, her words were no more than a whisper. "Do you think my dad has been through the same thing?"

It was the one question I had hoped she wouldn't ask. I gave her an empathetic look and said, "It's possible."

"Your grandpa and great-grandpa most likely did too," Austin said.

"Now that you know what's going on, you can stop it all… right?" Her voice was so full of hope that it hurt to break the news to her. I almost chickened out, but she deserved answers.

"There are still things we don't know about what goes on in that room. I think it would be beneficial to know what *really* happened the night Valerie died." I gave Sam an apologetic look. "The pieces just aren't fitting together yet."

I died a little inside as all hope drained from her face, and sheer disappointment took its place. "What's the plan then?"

"Well, it looks like we have to find Warren," Austin said.

"How?"

"With more research," I groaned, letting my head drop into my hands.

Sam eyed us suspiciously. "How can you track him down when the police have never been able to?"

I grinned smugly. "We have our ways."

"Beisdes, they probably gave up the search years ago," Austin added. "Long before the technology we have now."

"The library won't be useful this time," I said. "We'll do everything here on our laptops."

"If we go into the office, I can use the computer in there to help out," Sam offered.

Austin and I agreed to let her help. We picked up our laptops and followed her downstairs to the office behind the front desk. The room was larger than I had expected. There was a dark brown antique desk along the wall opposite the door, with a computer that looked relatively new. One of those gigantic filing cabinets you see in doctor's offices stood to the left of the desk, and to the right were the boxes Sam and I had gone through the day before. A single bookcase, packed tight with dusty old books, stood just inside the door.

There were no windows in the office which made it rather stuffy with three people in it. We opted to leave the door open for some airflow. Sam sat at the desk and booted up the computer while Austin and I sat on the floor, backs against the wall, with our laptops.

We were fully aware that Sam probably knew little to nothing about tracking someone down, but we gave her props for trying. At least Austin and I were experts in the matter… or so we thought. Needless to say, we were beyond frustrated when an hour had passed and zero progress had been made.

"I've looked at every type of record out there for a Warren Williams—birth and death certificates, police records, marriage records, you name it—and none of the results come close to matching him," I said, throwing my hands out to the side in frustration, and accidentally hitting Austin in the face.

"Well shit, you don't have to take it out on me," he grumbled, rubbing his cheek.

I gave him a sheepish, apologetic look and mouthed a quiet *oops*.

"Maybe there's not any records for him," Sam said.

"That's impossible," Austin told her. "Birth certificates were required by the time he would've been born, so there would at least be that floating around out there somewhere."

"Yes, that's true," Sam agreed. "But I took a genealogy course in college and actually learned a thing or two. Like in some cases, only the last name was written on the birth certificate. The first name would either be left blank or have the gender of the baby.

"And unless he's dead or has been in trouble with the law any other time, we won't find a death or police record for him," I finished for her.

She nodded. "Exactly."

"But how would he get around census records?" I knitted my brow thoughtfully.

"An alias," Austin replied. "It's technically illegal. But the census cares more about counting heads than proving who they really are."

"Huh," I said, feeling only slightly embarrassed that I didn't know that.

"So, based on the assumption that absolutely no records exist under his name, how do we find him?" Sam asked inquisitively.

I looked at Austin, hoping he knew the answer. But he remained silent.

Leaning my head back against the wall, I let out a long, exasperated sigh. "It'd be nice if someone could at least point us in the right direction."

As if on cue, a loud *bang!* came from across the room. All three of us jumped and whipped around to look. The door had slammed shut despite there not being any breeze. I opened my mouth to ask how the hell that happened when my attention was pulled elsewhere. A single book was now laying on the floor near the bookcase. Austin and I rose to our feet to investigate.

"That's weird," I said, picking up the book. I glanced at the bookcase and spotted the empty slot where it once was.

"What's it say?" Austin asked as he stepped closer to me.

"The Foster Family History," I read out loud.

Sam stood next to us and said, "I've never seen this book before."

I opened it and slowly flipped through the pages. The first few talked about the history of the bed-and-breakfast—how Leonard Foster had bought the abandoned building and turned it into the place it is today. It even included the other unsuccessful attempts of running the business, but conveniently failed to mention why it was shut down each time.

The handwriting changed throughout the pages from various people writing in it over time. I searched the book for a date it may have been started, but I couldn't find any. Judging by the yellowed pages, it had been around for a quite a while.

At the center of the book, the pages folded out to reveal a large family tree. It had been filled in recently enough that Sam's name was scribbled near the roots.

"What does that say?" Sam pointed to a bit of writing next to Leonard's name on the second tier from the top.

I moved the book closer to my face and squinted. "I can't tell. It's all smudged."

I folded the page up again and moved on. Toward the end of the book were old Polaroid headshots of each family member with their names written on the white strip at the bottom. Each photo was placed in a separate slot of a plastic protective sleeve.

"Wait, what's that?" Austin asked as he grabbed the corner of something sticking out from behind Leonard's photo.

He pulled it out, revealing another Polaroid. I inhaled sharply as I instantly recognized the faces smiling back at me. It was the same photo I'd seen of Valerie and Warren in the article about her death. I snatched it from Austin's hand and flipped it over. The back of the photo read: *To my brother Leonard. With love, Warren.*

"Oh my god," I breathed.

Sam leaned in closer to read the chicken scratch. "I thought Great-Grandpa Leonard was an only child."

"Apparently not," Austin said, sounding as baffled as I felt.

"The police report said the owner didn't know the couple weren't married." I paced back and forth as I thought out loud. "Leonard was the owner. He lied."

"Which means it's safe to assume that he knew about the murder and kept the police from finding any evidence in the master suite," Austin added.

"And I bet he played a role in making sure Warren was never found," I finished.

Sam looked at me questioningly. "But he died years ago. Wouldn't they have found Warren once he was no longer in the way?"

I stared off into the distance as the wheels in my head kept turning. "Not if he passed his dirty work onto someone else."

"It had to be someone with the ability to keep police from finding the hidden evidence in the room all these years," Austin said. "And I'm sure it wasn't an easy task once more and more people started dying."

"My grandpa and my aunt," Sam said. Then she met my gaze. "And now my dad. That's what Valerie was trying to tell us. They've been hiding the evidence. They know something!"

I nodded in agreement. When I had asked Valerie where I could find information about Warren, she pointed toward Mike, who was watching us from the window of his room—the master suite. The room where tragedies happen, yet evidence is never found. The only room that hadn't been renovated.

"That could be why she's going after your family," Austin told her. "They know about Warren and haven't done anything about it which makes them just as bad as he is."

"Well, good news," I announced as I returned the book to its proper spot. "Finding Warren is *exactly* what we need to do."

CHAPTER FIFTEEN

Austin narrowed his eyes at me. "Are you sure about that?"

"About ninety-five percent sure," I said confidently. "Valerie is the one that opened the article about her own death for me to see. Then she let me know that Mike knows about Warren. And now we find this book chock-full of information that mysteriously wandered off the bookcase and onto the floor." I held my arms open. "I mean, come on! It's obvious she's trying to tell us what to do here."

Austin nodded in agreement. "If it wasn't the solution, she wouldn't be directing us to him."

"Exactly."

"But if she wants you guys to find Warren, then why doesn't she let my dad share any information with you?" Sam asked.

Her question was valid, and somehow I knew the answer. "I think she's only keeping Mike from telling us what she's doing to him. He just refuses to share anything else."

"Because he'd be betraying his own family and throwing everyone under the bus if he was the cause of the police finding Warren," Austin said. "So he's the one choosing to keep that part to himself—not Valerie telling him to. I think it's time we confront him, find Warren, and the police handle the rest."

"Turning Warren in won't end this." The words came out without me even realizing. It was like my subconscious had come to that conclusion and failed to alert me before spilling it out. "If it was a matter of seeing him punished along with those who protected him all these years, then she wouldn't be going after all the other guys in that room. She wants us to bring him here—she wants *revenge*."

"So you're saying we have to drag an old man here for his dead fiancée to brutally murder him as an act of revenge?" Austin asked, then shook his head in disbelief. "No. I can't do that. There has to be some other way."

"What other ideas do you have, then?" I questioned.

He rubbed the back of his neck while Sam knitted her brows. They were both stumped.

"Look, why don't we just focus on finding Warren and then go from there?" Austin suggested finally.

"Deal," I said. "But first we have to get Mike to tell us where he is."

"Tonight we can stay up to watch the camera," Austin said. "Tomorrow we'll demand that he share everything he knows."

"What if he still refuses to tell you anything?" Sam asked.

Austin shrugged. "We got this far on our own. I'm sure we could find Warren without his help. Once Mike realizes that, it won't do him any good to keep things a secret."

"Sounds like a plan to me," I said.

"Me too," Sam agreed.

The three of us went back to our room and decided to play some card games to pass the time. It was bound to be a long night. We were chowing down on snacks and having a good ol' time when Austin's phone started emitting strange sounds. He yanked the phone off the tripod and turned it so we could all see the live camera footage from Mike's room.

Mike was sitting on the edge of his bed, looking tense and uncomfortable. Valerie was standing in front of him. But something about her was different. I leaned in closer to see better.

"Oh my goodness," I breathed in amazement. "She's beautiful."

Though she was still naked, Valerie looked alive and well. No wounds. No decaying flesh. Just smooth, flawless ivory skin. Her dark, silky hair fell in knot-free waves. If I hadn't known any better, I would've thought the person I'd seen in the woods the day before had been a figment of my imagination.

"I-Is she alive?" Sam stammered, her eyes wide with disbelief.

"No," Austin said without looking away from the screen. "Spirits have the ability to show themselves in different ways—depending on what their intentions are. Sometimes they appear alive and act innocent to lure someone into a bad situation, or they may appear dead to instill fear."

"Val," Mike's soft-spoken voice barely picked up on the camera. "We're going to get caught. You can't do this while they're here."

Valerie cupped his face between her hands, staring down into his eyes. His body went limp, as if he were put in a trance. Lowering her face to his, she kissed him firmly on the lips. As if he'd been set to autopilot, Mike's arms wrapped around her slim, naked waist, pulling her in closer.

Then with a speed so fast the camera blurred, Valerie had him pinned down on the bed. Bile rose in the back of my throat as I watched her grind against him. The moan-grunt noise Sam and I heard before echoed around us as it both blared through the speaker and drifted down the hall to our room.

Please, for the love of God, make it stop!

"I have to stop this," Austin said as if he were the Almighty himself answering my silent prayer. He got to his feet quickly and rushed to the door.

"No!" I screeched as I ran after him and pulled him back to me. "She'll go after you next!"

He turned to face me, giving me one of his famous cocky grins. "Let her try."

"Austin, this isn't a joke. You'll get yourself killed!" I shouted in exasperation. "I won't let you go in there."

"Well, someone has to put a stop to it," he said firmly.

"You're right," I said flatly. Then I shoved him to the side and reached for the doorknob. "I'll do it."

"Hell no you won't!" he snapped as he gripped my forearm.

"I've met Valerie," I reminded him, feeling my body heat up with rising anger. "She won't hurt me. Besides, this is *my* case. Not yours. Now let go so I can do my damn job."

I yanked my arm out of his grasp, throwing him a cold glare. Austin pressed his lips into a thin line, holding back any further protest. He raked a hand through his hair and lifted his face heavenward. A mix of fury and fear tightened every muscle in his body as he fought the urge to stop me.

"Fine," he hissed through gritted teeth. "But I'm watching the cameras. If anything starts to go wrong…"

"I'll go with her," Sam piped up. "But we need to hurry. This never lasts long."

"Let's go," I said.

As we rushed out of the room, I heard Austin mutter angrily to himself. Knowing I'd upset him like that absolutely tore me to pieces. But there was a job to be done and his safety meant everything to me. Hurt feelings could be fixed. But losing him…

"Are you ready?" I asked Sam, breaking out of my own thoughts as he approached Mike's room.

"No." Her voice shook with fear. "But let's get it over with."

I turned the knob, thankful that it was unlocked, and flung the door open. Valerie still had Mike pinned to the bed and was tearing his clothes off of him, ripping them to shreds. I wrinkled my nose at the sight. That wasn't an image I wanted embedded in my mind.

"Valerie, stop!" I yelled. But she completely ignored me. I tried again. "Valerie!"

As I approached her, fully intending to physically stop her, she whipped around to face me. Her face softened slightly, and I sighed with relief, thinking that I'd gained her trust enough before to have a calm conversation with her now. But then, in the blink of an eye, she changed to the rotting, dead version of herself. Her dark sunken eyes narrowed at me as she let out a low, menacing growl.

"Oh, cut it out," I snapped, feeling a little too confident and cocky for the situation. "You don't scare me one bit." Hey, I never claimed to be the brightest Crayola in the pack.

Valerie stretched one arm out toward me, then with a simple flick of her wrist, and invisible force threw me backward off my feet. I collided with the wall behind me, causing the air to leave my lungs in a rush. Pain radiated throughout my body and I grimaced. I tried to move, but the force kept me pressed tight against the wall.

"Ava!" I heard Austin shout from down the hall.

Valerie turned slightly until she faced the door, then flicked her wrist again. It slammed shut and the lock clicked into place.

Within seconds, Austin's voice came through the other side as he jiggled the knob wildly. "Open the door!"

Sam started to move to let him in, but the dead girl flashed her a warning glare, stopping her in her tracks. Knowing that Austin was safe in the hall granted me the ability to clear my mind and think of a way out of this situation.

"You don't want to do this." My voice was strained as the force pinning me in place made it difficult to breathe, let alone speak. "Remember who the real enemy is, Valerie."

The anger in her eyes faded ever so slightly, but the hold she had on me did not. I narrowed my eyes and let frustration and anger take over. "You want me to find Warren, don't you?" Her body jerked as if a jolt of electricity had shot through it—whether it was from my tone or the mention of her killer. She nodded slowly. "Then you have to let me go! I can't do anything while pinned to a damn wall."

Valerie dropped her arm, releasing the force and causing me to fall on my butt. I kept my eyes locked on hers as I got back on my feet.

"You also need to leave our source of information alone," I told her as I waved a hand toward Mike, who was giving me that deer in the headlights look. "Promise me you'll leave him alone so I can find Warren for you."

She glanced over her shoulder at Mike, then looked back at me. Her face remained guarded as she took a few steps in my direction. A tinge of fear crept through me as she got closer.

She stopped at arm's length away and reached a hand out toward me. My muscles clenched as I braced myself for the worst. I flinched when her ice-cold hand wrapped around mine. Chills raced through my body as the words *I promise* whispered through my head. I gasped loudly, but before I could say anything else, Valerie vanished into thin air.

CHAPTER SIXTEEN

Sam rushed to Mike's side, helping him sit upright again. His blazer lay at the foot of the bed, and the white shirt he wore underneath had been torn to pieces, exposing most of his torso. Luckily, his pants remained on and mostly intact. Things would've taken a seriously awkward turn otherwise.

"Let's get him to our room," I told Sam.

As she helped Mike to his feet, I opened the door and promptly walked into a brick wall named Austin.

"Ava," he breathed as he wrapped his arms tight around me. "Are you okay?"

"Yes," I mumbled against his chest. His body relaxed slightly, but his heart still pounded heavily.

He kept one arm around my waist as the four of us retreated down the hall to our room. Sam wheeled the desk chair over to the bed for Mike to sit in. She stood behind him, her hands resting on his trembling shoulders. Austin and I sat on the edge of the bed in front of him.

"We have some questions for you, and you must be completely honest with us," I told Mike. He swallowed hard, then nodded. "Not long after you opened this place, Valerie gave you a choice, didn't she?"

Mike jerked in surprise. He didn't expect me to know so much. I fought back a small, victorious smile. *You can't lie to us anymore now.*

"And you chose to live," Austin continued for me.

Mike narrowed his eyes at Austin, like he couldn't believe there was ever another option. "Of course. What kind of father would I be if I willingly left my daughter all alone in this world?" Then he turned to look up at Sam. "I've always been there for you, and I always will be."

Sam's eyes glistened with unshed tears as she flashed her dad a sad half-smile. The look in her eyes said she appreciated his sacrifice to remain on earth with her... but at what cost? After all, Steve had done the same thing, and look where he ended up.

"Do you know who Warren Williams is?" Austin asked, putting a halt to the bittersweet father-daughter moment.

Mike sighed in defeat. "Yes. He was Valerie's fiancé."

"And Leonard's brother," I added. Then I cocked my head to the side and studied him closely. "But you already knew that, didn't you?"

"Half brother," Mike corrected me.

I gave him a smug look. The family history book did not mention Warren being a half brother. Now there was no doubt in my mind Mike had all the answers we were looking for.

"Where is he now?" I asked.

"I don't know," he replied. "He and Leonard had written letters to each other after he ran off, but only one had a return address." A crease formed on his forehead as he thought. "I think it was from somewhere in Utah. But that was a long time ago."

Austin looked down his nose at Mike. "How do you know about the letters?"

"I found them hidden in the storage room when I was cleaning it out for renovations."

"Is there anything else you know about him that could help us track him down?" I asked as we came to the end of our little midnight interrogation.

Mike opened his mouth to speak, then closed it again. Inner turmoil reflected in his eyes as he tried to decide whether he should share more—to disobey the wishes of his grandfather.

Sam stepped around to look at him, staring deep into his eyes, pleading with him to tell us what he knows. "Dad, Valerie killed people before and will do it again. Finding Warren is one step closer to stopping her."

Understanding registered on his face. His gaze flicked back to Austin and me. "His name isn't Warren Williams anymore. It's Edward Morris."

I blinked in surprise. That's why we couldn't find any records for him. Warren Williams really didn't exist anymore.

"And you're certain you don't know where he is?" Austin asked again.

"I give you my word," Mike assured him evenly.

Austin gave him a short nod and said, "Thank you for sharing what you know. You may return to your room now."

"I'll walk him back," Sam offered. Before leaving the room, she added, "And if you don't mind, I'd like to sleep in my own room tonight. This floor is killing my body."

"That's fine," I told her. "You're not in danger here."

"Well, then, I'll see you two in the morning. Goodnight."

Then her and Mike stepped into the hall, closing the door behind them.

I felt gross after my little encounter with the dead, so I opted for a quick shower. Afterward, I plopped down on the bed with my laptop, eager to see where the newfound information on Warren—I mean Edward—took me. The end to all of this felt so close yet so far.

A few minutes into my investigation, Austin emerged from the bathroom, towel-drying his blond hair. I mentally cursed him for distracting me by being shirtless again. Tossing the towel off to the side, he scooped up his laptop and joined me in the search.

Occasionally, my eyes would drift to the side, admiring his godlike figure. On the third time, I had to bite my lip to keep from smiling.

Keeping his eyes on the screen of his laptop, Austin chuckled softly. "If it makes you feel any better, I do it too."

"Do what?" I asked innocently.

"Check you out," he teased. One corner of his mouth tilted up in a cocky smirk. "I'm just better at hiding it."

My face flamed with embarrassment as he turned those deep blue eyes on me. Feeling the need to reply with words, I opened my mouth. But all that came out were a bunch of random sounds as I lost all ability to speak English.

"I can't help it," he said, shrugging like it was no big deal. "You're beautiful."

"Thanks," I muttered sheepishly. Inside, my mind was screaming *oh my goodness!* like an infatuated teenager who just found out the hottest, most popular guy in school knows her name.

But unlike the teenager invading my thoughts, I was not going to blow his words out of proportion. After all, friends complement each other. No big deal… right?

I could practically see my conscience rolling her eyes inside my head. *Please, just please with this denial crap.*

Austin had already returned his focus to his work, as if nothing happened. I mentally shook myself and followed his lead. Now was not the time to be thinking about feelings and love and…

Who the hell said anything about love?

Either way, there was a job to be done, and I needed to concentrate on it.

A couple of hours passed by, and our hopes of finding anything were dwindling down. Somehow, knowing Warren's new name wasn't making our task any easier like we thought it would. We found people so easily in the past, so why was it a struggle now?

"Anything yet?" I asked Austin around a big yawn.

"No." He rubbed his face, looking tired and frustrated. Setting his laptop aside, he said, "But we need some sleep."

"Go ahead. I'll continue searching," I said.

He looked heavenward and reached for his laptop again. I grabbed his arm to stop him. "What are you doing?"

"Well, I'm not gonna make you do all the work by yourself."

"No, no." I grinned as I patted his head gently. "You need to get some sleep."

"Fine," he said on a dramatic sigh.

He scooted closer to me and rested his head on my shoulder, letting out a loud fake snore. I burst out laughing. Still keeping his eyes closed, he hushed me. "You're interrupting my sleep."

Rolling my eyes, I turned back to the laptop. It wasn't long until Austin really did fall asleep with his head still on my shoulder. Eventually, he maneuvered himself onto his side with his back to me. Then I relocated to the desk so I wouldn't disturb him.

More hours had come and gone without me realizing it until the light of the rising sun began to fill the room. No matter where I looked, I came up empty handed. It really was as if the guy had fallen off the face of the earth.

Groaning in frustration, I stood up and suddenly realized how stiff my whole body had become. I circled around the room, trying to get my joints working again. At the window, I peered outside. The morning sun lit up the edge of the woods, making it seem more welcoming than usual.

The sound of the bed creaking caught my attention. I turned to see Austin pulling himself upright.

"You're still awake?" he asked groggily.

"Yeah." I faced the window again.

He got up and stood beside me. "You need to sleep."

"No. I need to finish this case and go home," I corrected him.

"Why are you so determined?"

I threw him a sideways glare. "This isn't just someone's grandma refusing to leave her poor family behind. People have died, Austin. If I don't stop it..." I paused, afraid to speak the truth of what would happen if I failed to help Valerie find peace. My next words were barely a whisper. "I won't let another family perish because of me."

Austin spun me around and pulled me into a giant bear hug. "It wasn't your fault."

"I could've done more."

"You don't know that. Demons are hard to get rid of." He sighed, then quietly added, "Just like vengeful spirits."

I clung to him a moment longer, then pulled away. He looked down at me with a smile that sent my pulse soaring. HIs eyes roamed my face slowly, like he was getting ready to...

Then he stepped back, running his fingers through his hair nervously. He cleared his throat, then said, "How about I continue the search while you sleep?"

"I'm fine. I've got this," I replied.

"Ava, you're going to crash and burn soon."

I crossed my arms stubbornly. "That sounds like my problem, not yours."

"Look." His voice was thick with aggravation. "I came here to help you. Not to watch you destroy yourself doing it all on your own."

Refusing to stand down, I brushed past him and returned to the desk. He mumbled something under his breath, though I couldn't quite make it out. In the reflection of my screen, I saw him watching me. A couple of minutes later, he crouched beside me, resting a hand on my arm.

"I'm sorry," he said softly. "I just care a lot about you, alright? I don't want to see anything bad happen to you."

I huffed, hating my inability to stay mad at him. "I care about you too."

"I know," he said, flashing me an adorable smirk that automatically made me smile in return. Then he sat on the foot of the bed. "So what have you come up with?"

"A whole lot of nothing." I spun the chair around to face him. "I've searched all kinds of records for Edward Morris. There's nothing that matches him. It's like he doesn't exist."

Austin cocked a brow and said, "Maybe Edward Morris *doesn't* exist."

I blinked in confusion. That boy made little to no sense sometimes.

"What I mean is, maybe he didn't legally change his name. It's super easy to get by in life with an alias unless it involves legal documents."

I slowly moved my head up and down as I started to understand. Then a flaw in his thought process occurred to me. "Legal documents are required to get a home, a job, a car… anything for basic living. How would he do that without people knowing who he is?"

"I'm sure he's retired by now, and background checks for jobs weren't as common back in his early days," Austin explained. "As for a car and home, they're not going to run a background check to look for outstanding warrants. Nor will anyone recognize his name— especially in another state, years after Valerie's murder had been forgotten."

"There should be some public record out there connecting him to a physical location if the home is in his name," I said.

"Maybe it's not," Austin countered. "Someone else could've put it under their name to protect his identity."

I raised a brow and crossed my arms over my chest. "Someone like Leonard Foster?"

"Doubtful, since he's… you know… *dead*," he pointed out. "But it could still be in the family."

I chewed my lip thoughtfully. "Mike seemed to genuinely not know his whereabouts. I'm sure it's not in his name."

"Mike isn't the only Foster still alive, though… is he?"

CHAPTER SEVENTEEN

"My aunt?" Sam's mouth gaped open in shock.

After determining Warren's home may be under another relative's name, Austin and I went downstairs to find Sam and Mike. They were deep in conversation with each other as we approached. Then they gave us identical looks of hope—clearly expecting some better news than we had to offer. I filled them in on our findings.

"She's the only other Foster alive that's most likely aware of the situation," I explained. "There's no way she ran this place without knowing something about Valerie and Warren."

"I suppose you're right," Mike admitted. "But are you sure there's no way to find him without getting in touch with her? My sister can be a little… challenging."

Austin shook his head. "We've exhausted all other options."

Mike gave a short nod of understanding. "Can I at least have some time to think of a way to approach her about this? Surely there's a reason she never shared it with me before."

"We'll give you until tomorrow," I said. "In the meantime, we'll continue to search on our own. The sooner you talk to her, the better."

"Understood."

As Austin and I headed for the staircase, Sam piped up. "Hang on a second." She disappeared into the office then emerged a few seconds later with a paper in her hand. "I couldn't sleep very well, so I figured I'd do some more searching on my own. I found this." She handed the paper to me. "It might be nothing, but it's all I could find."

Austin leaned in closer to me as we examined the paper together. It was an article about a "local hero" who saved a woman who was being raped by her ex-boyfriend. At the bottom of the page was a photo of an elderly man with the name Edward Morris printed in small letters below it.

Sam handed me the photo of Valerie and Warren that was found in the family history book. I held the old photo beside the article to do a side-by-side comparison.

"He's aged, but that's definitely him," Austin murmured beside me.

"So he's a hero for saving a woman from the same fate he gave his fiancée." I scoffed at the irony. Then I looked at Sam. "What town was this in?"

"West Plains, Missouri. Approximately three hours away," she replied matter-of-factly. "I had a strong feeling it was him, so I took the liberty of searching the location to save you time."

I scanned the paper again until I found a date. "This is from a few years ago. Would he still be there?"

"It's worth checking out," Austin said.

"Even if he isn't there, it's a small town. I'm sure someone might remember him and may even know where he's at now," Mike added.

I looked at Austin. "When should we go?"

"How about today?"

I could feel exhaustion start to set in, but I agreed to the last-minute trip anyway. We didn't waste any time gathering the things we'd need: printouts of reports, news articles, and Austin's trusty voice recorder.

"Are you going to be okay here?" I asked Sam as we passed through the lobby.

She smiled confidently and nodded. "I'll be fine. Please, go put an end to all of this."

Austin and I jumped in his car and hit the road. Gray clouds loomed overhead the closer we got to the Arkansas-Missouri border. I hoped the darkness forming wasn't an omen of some kind. Somewhere along the way, the pitter patter of raindrops on the windshield lulled me to sleep.

When I opened my eyes again, Austin was turning the car into the parking lot of the West Plains Police Department. He told me to wait in the car while he went inside. A few minutes later, he returned with a slip of paper in his hand.

"What's that?" I asked as he climbed into the driver's seat.

He smirked. "One address for a Ms. Amanda Foster."

"So the home really is under Sam's aunt's name, huh?"

"Apparently so." He shrugged, then input the address into the GPS.

"How did you manage to get them to pass you an address like that?" I asked curiously.

Austin flashed me a cocky grin and winked as he backed out of the parking spot.

Yeah, that look would make me hand you anything you wanted too.

My face instantly flushed at the thought. The soft chuckle he let out made me wonder if he could really read my mind at times. God, I'd keel over and die from embarrassment if he could.

Before long, he steered the Lexus into the driveway of a tiny, rundown house. What appeared to have once been clean, white siding had turned a nasty green-brown color. The roof over the porch had begun to sag in the middle, and a short set of janky wooden steps led up to the front door.

"This is it," Austin announced as he cut the engine and took in our surroundings.

"Are you sure?" I asked, wrinkling my nose with uncertainty.

He nodded in response. As I got out of the car, I folded the copies of the police and autopsy reports I'd brought and shoved them into my back pocket. Then we headed toward the door. The wooden boards of the porch creaked and groaned under my feet, threatening to collapse at any moment.

Austin took the recorder out of his pocket long enough to hit the record button, then slipped it back in. There was a good chance Warren would not agree to being recorded if asked, but we needed the conversation for future reference, so we had to be sneaky about it.

Then Austin knocked on the door and waited. When no one answered, he knocked a little louder. This time we heard someone moving around inside the house. He was just getting ready to knock again when the door slowly opened.

An elderly man appeared in the doorway wearing a red-and-black plaid button-down shirt that was tucked neatly into his jeans. His gray hair was combed over to hide the fact it had thinned out over the years. Though his face had filled with wrinkles and the happy twinkle in his eyes was long gone, I knew without a doubt this was the man we'd worked so hard to find.

"Good afternoon, sir," Austin greeted him. "Are you Edward Morris?"

The man looked back and forth between us, hesitant to give a straight answer. "Who's asking?"

"I'm Austin and this is Ava. We're friends of the Foster family."

As soon as he said the family name, the man's eyes widened with a mixture of surprise and horror. "What do you want?"

"We have some questions about an incident that occurred many years ago," Austin replied evenly. "Just a few minutes of your time is all we need."

"I know nothing," the man hissed as he retreated inside the house.

Acting quickly, I shoved my foot into the closing gap, preventing him from shutting the door all the way.

"On the contrary," I said, narrowing my eyes at him. "I think you know a lot... *Warren.*"

His jaw dropped the instant I spoke his real name. There was no way he'd refuse to talk to us now. After all, we knew enough to turn him in if we wanted to. What would be the harm in telling us a little more?

"We're not here to get you in trouble," Austin assured him. "We just want some answers."

Warren hesitated for a moment, then stepped aside, opening the door all the way. He waved us inside, then shut the door behind us.

The inside was in so much better shape than the outside I almost couldn't believe we'd entered the same house. The basic white walls were covered with photos and shelves filled with knickknacks. A large area rug was centered in the middle of the room. The gray sofa and matching chairs were angled to face a flat screen television that sat on a wooden stand in the corner of the room.

"Have a seat," Warren said, pointing toward the sofa.

Austin and I sat, instantly sinking into the squishy cushions. Warren sat in the chair and turned his body slightly to face us. He stared at us intently, which we took as our cue to begin the discussion.

"So you're really Leonard's brother," Austin said.

"Half brother," Warren corrected him.

"Why wasn't the family aware of your relation?"

"My father had an affair with my mother," he explained. "Something of that nature was viewed as the devil's work. They tried hard to hide my existence from the Foster's, with the exception of Leonard. My last name, Williams, was taken from my mother."

Now that Austin and I were there, it seemed as if we were both unsure about what answers we were really seeking to make all well again with Valerie. Not to mention the fear of making Warren mad and going back to Arkansas empty-handed lingered in the air around us.

Sensing our uncertainty, Warren looked at us knowingly. "But you didn't come all this way to ask about my family, did you?"

"No, sir," I replied truthfully.

"You're here to find out about *her*."

It wasn't a question, but I answered anyway. "Yes, sir. We want to know what happened."

"Haven't you seen the new reports?" he questioned.

"We want to know what *really* happened," I emphasized.

Warren nodded, knowing I meant we wanted his recollection of that awful night in 1958. Not the story that had been fabricated by authorities who had nothing to go off of except assumptions and biased opinions. He stared down at his lap. A moment of silence passed before he lifted his head again to tell us the devastating story of the night Valerie Evans died.

"Valerie and I were high school sweethearts. She was the daughter of a preacher and I was just a rebellious bastard child who had fallen head over heels for someone way out of my league. Her parents tried to tear us apart many times. The day after she turned eighteen, I proposed to her. Boy, her old man sure hated that." Warren let out a small chuckle at the memory.

"She couldn't stand anymore of her parents bickering over the proposal, so she asked me to take her away for a couple of days while they calmed down. Leonard was willing to let us stay at his bed-and-breakfast for a weekend—in secret, of course. He had reserved the master suite just for us. It was late when we arrived, but Leonard asked for my help with something. While I assisted him, Val went up to the room. She hadn't been up there for more than an hour by the time I joined her. The lights were turned off, but the moon shined in enough for me to see her." Warren's face shifted to a look of concern, as if mimicking the expression he'd had that night more than sixty years ago.

"She was sitting on the bed… naked. I walked over to the nightstand and picked up the empty bottle of wine Leonard had left us as a congratulatory gift. Val had never had even a sip of alcohol before that night, yet she drank the entire bottle herself within an hour.

"She asked me to make love to her for the first time." He shook his head in bewilderment. "Believe me, I wanted to, but I refused because she was drunk. My momma raised me right—taught me how to treat a woman with respect. I thought I was doing the right thing, but she was mad at me. I'd never upset her like that before."

I gave him a sad half-smile. "You really did do the right thing, though."

"I know," he said quietly. Then he cleared his throat and continued. "Then she forced herself on me and tried to undress me. It came to the point I had to use a little force to escape her. In the struggle, one of us must've knocked the wine bottle off the nightstand and the glass shattered everywhere."

The memory of Austin and me finding tiny shards of glass embedded in the scratch marks on the hardwood floor flashed through my mind. *That's one piece of the puzzle figured out.*

"I tried to leave the room, but she grabbed me. Her unusual reaction threw me off guard so much she managed to overtake me, slamming me into the wall." He pointed toward his back. "There's still a scar on my shoulder blade from the wall crumbling under the impact and scratching me. Those damn walls were so thin," he grumbled.

That's how the dent in the wall got there. Now all that was missing was how the blood got there. And, of course, how Valerie died.

"Even though I felt in danger, I did everything I could to not hurt her. But then she started punching me and wouldn't let me go."

Warren stopped to take some deep breaths, trying to collect himself before continuing. His eyes had begun to shimmer with tears.

"Take your time," I said gently.

He sat up straighter and continued recounting the events of that night. "I grabbed her arms and pushed her away. I didn't take into account that her balance was no good since she was drunk. She ended up stumbling backward and falling. Then everything was quiet. I waited a minute, thinking she'd move or say something. When she didn't, I turned the light on and the sight was… unbearable." His voice broke as the tears finally flowed over, pouring in steady streams down his cheeks. "She'd fallen on the broken glass and blood was forming on the floor from underneath her. I called her name and shook her, but she didn't react."

"What did you do when you saw what had happened?" Austin asked.

"I panicked. I ran to find Leonard. Big brothers always know what to do."

Tilting my head in curiosity, I asked, "Was it his idea to hide the body?"

Warren nodded. "When we got back to the room and saw she hadn't moved at all, we knew she was dead. Leonard said we needed to get rid of the body and pretend nothing ever happened. I was the only person he had left in his life at the time, so he was willing to go to the extreme to protect me."

"How did you dispose of the body?" I asked, wanting to know how well it matched the police reports.

"We wrapped her in a blanket and carried her out into the woods. Leonard thought it was a good idea to pile some brush over her to reduce the chances of wild animals dragging her body off to be discovered," he replied.

I saw Austin cringe out of the corner of my eye, disturbed by the unpleasant mental image. Then he asked, "Why did you remain hidden from the world instead of coming clean and accepting the punishment after Leonard passed away?"

Warren narrowed his eyes at Austin. "Son, hiding from the world *is* my punishment."

"How?"

"Back then, I might've been sentenced to death for what I did," Warren replied. "The death penalty would've been the easy way out. I deserve to live the rest of my life with the guilt and regret of knowing I killed the love of my life. That's far worse than the law could've ever done to me."

"If you had reported her death to the cops right away, wouldn't they have counted it as self=defense on your part?" I asked.

"A judge would've never seen it that way," Warren stated, shaking his head. "If a woman hurts a man in an altercation, it's self-defense and she's praised for it. But nobody believes that a *real* man would have to defend himself against a woman. He's seen as weak if he speaks of a woman abusing him, and he's seen as an abuser if he uses self-defense and hurts her in the process. It's a lose-lose situation."

I thought back to the police report and how they automatically assume Valerie had been sexually assaulted based on the fact she was naked and had been at The Foster House with a man. A decision was set in their mind right from the beginning based on nothing but stereotypes and highly opinionated authorities. Warren would not have stood a chance in court.

Then I recalled something else from the police report—a major flaw between stories.

"How long after the incident did you take her into the woods?" I asked, backtracking just a little bit. Austin looked over at me, his face a giant question mark.

"I don't know." Warren shrugged. "Maybe an hour. We worked fast."

A knot formed in my stomach as I realized that I knew something he didn't know about that night. "Did you ever listen to or read the reports when she was found?"

He shook his head. "Leonard told me she'd been found, but I never wanted to know any details. I felt it would be better that way."

"Well, I think there's something you should know." I shifted uncomfortably in my seat as I began to make his living nightmare even worse. "When they found her, she wasn't where you had left her."

Warren's forehead wrinkled in confusion. "Did an animal get to her?"

"No." I shook my head. "She moved on her own."

"That's impossible," he breathed in disbelief. "She was dead!"

I took a deep inhale and continued. "When they did the autopsy, they found she had died from a brain hemorrhage. The severity of it would've taken several hours to kill her—even faster when exertion is used."

"Like the exertion used to escape a blanket and a pile of brush," Austin added.

"What are you saying?" Warren asked slowly.

I glanced nervously at Austin and he nodded for me to break the news.

"Valerie was still alive when you hid her body."

CHAPTER EIGHTEEN

The silence was deafening as Warren processed my words. A somber expression crossed his face and his eyes became distant.

"That can't be," he whispered. "There was too much blood, and she didn't move the whole time. She wasn't responding to anything."

"She hit her head when she fell which knocked her unconscious and caused the hemorrhage," Austin explained softly.

"Here," I said as I pulled out the folded reports and passed them to Warren. "These are the official police and autopsy reports."

He took the papers and studied them closely. As he processed the truth of the matter, he burst into tears once again. Austin and I sat in silence, allowing him to take a moment to grieve.

"You and Leonard kept in touch after everything, right?" Austin asked once Warren had collected himself again.

Warren nodded as he pulled a handkerchief from his pocket and wiped his face. "He'd send letters to me, being careful not to include my name or any hints of my location."

"Did you know about his suicide?" Austin asked.

"He'd sent me a letter about a week before it happened. More deaths had happened there and he started to get questioned a lot. He was afraid he'd end up breaking down and telling the truth about what happened to Val."

"So he took his own life to save yours," I said, so quietly I didn't think anyone even heard me. But Warren looked at me with sad eyes and gave a slow nod.

Then I asked, "Are you aware of what has happened at The Foster house since then?"

"I've seen the news reports on occasion."

"We need your help putting an end to all these deaths," Austin said.

I could see the confusion on Warren's face, so I explained, "Valerie is the one committing these murders. Her spirit is trapped there and she's getting revenge for her own death. Once her spirit finds peace, all of this will come to an end."

"How could I possibly help with that?" Warren asked.

"If you confront her, you could make her understand what really happened that night. She has to know you were trying to protect yourself and never meant to hurt her," I said.

"Or you need to come clean to the police and accept the consequences," Austin added.

I stifled the urge to smack him. Just the day before, we were saying that tuning him in would *not* work.

"No," Warren said firmly without a second thought. "I can't bear to go back to that place. As for going to the police, my punishment isn't done. I won't do it."

"Refusing to do either one is putting more innocent lives at stake," Austin pointed out, trying to reason with him. "Including the lives of your own family."

"I said no!" Warren shouted, his face turning red with anger. I flinched at his outburst.

"Do you understand the danger you're putting people in?" Austin's voice was thick with fury.

Warren rose from the chair and headed to the door, flinging it wide open. "Get out of my home," he demanded through gritted teeth.

Austin and I stood up and headed to the door. As we passed Warren, I said, "Sir, I don't think—"

"Get out!" he spat angrily as he pointed a shaky finger out the door.

Once outside, I turned around to attempt to reason with him one last time, but before I could say a word, the door slammed shut in my face. I heard the faint click of the deadbolt sliding into place. I stood there for a few more seconds, heart pounding with anger, until a hand grasped my arm and dragged me to the car.

"How can someone be so stubborn?" I huffed as I climbed into the passenger seat.

Austin scoffed as he got in the other side. "You're one to talk."

I shot daggers at him. Now was not the time for smart-ass remarks. Upon seeing my face, he quickly pressed his lips together and turned his attention to the GPS.

What was supposed to be a relaxing and productive trip had turned out to be a stressful nightmare. About an hour had passed in complete silence. The dark clouds seemed to follow us, rain steadily pouring down.

My mind raced, wondering how someone could live with themselves knowing their own mistake had taken the lives of innocent people. Warren wasn't just punishing himself anymore—he was punishing everyone around him.

There has to be some other way…

"We did all we could," Austin said out loud, reading my mind… again.

I shook my head. "No, we didn't. We should've made him come with us."

"Ava," he said, glancing over at me like I'd lost every bit of my damn mind. "We can't force an old man into a car, drag him to another state, and throw him at the feet of his dead fiancée like some sort of sacrificial animal. I'm pretty sure that's illegal."

I sighed heavily, annoyed and frustrated. "Then let's just go to the cops."

"I only said that because I thought he would be more willing to face Valerie than the cops. You were right before—it won't work."

"Well, there has to be another way!" I said, raising my voice in frustration.

"Look, we learned the real story now. So let's compare that with everything else and go from there," Austin said calmly. He was way more level-headed than me in nearly every situation. Then he launched into a brief overview of the case. "Valerie is giving people a choice. If they reject her, she kills them. It seems to me that her spirit believes that rejection equals death. That's all she seems to be holding onto from that night—that she died after a rejection to sex."

"Spirits tend to see things as black or white," I said. "And alcohol really messes with a person's head. She probably doesn't even remember the incident correctly and doesn't realize she was in the wrong for forcing herself on Warren, just like she does with the other victims."

"Exactly. So if her victims reject her, she kills them before they get the chance to kill her like Warren did." He paused and shook his head, realizing how confusing his words sounded. "Either way, she needs to hear what really happened to find peace with the situation."

"But he won't confront her!" I yelled, throwing my arms out in frustration. "He'll save a random stranger but to hell with his own family and other innocent people."

"There is another way…" Austin started.

I stared at him, waiting to see where his thought process was going.

"The entire conversation was recorded. We could just play the recording for her."

"And by *we* you mean me, right?" I asked slowly. The look on his face gave the answer away before he even spoke.

"No. I mean you and me."

My stomach clenched as worry, fear, and panic exploded inside of me. "Oh, hell no. No way. Absolutely not!"

"Ava," he began calmly, trying to reason with me, but I cut him off.

"You'll get killed!"

He shrugged nonchalantly. "She hasn't done anything to me so far."

"So far," I repeated mockingly. "Just wait until you start siding with the man who killed her."

"I'll be fine."

"You've got to be kidding me," I groaned as I rolled my eyes, shaking my head in disbelief.

Frustration replaced the calmness in Austin's voice as he said, "Why the hell did you call me to help in the first place then?"

"Because I didn't know your life hung in the balance when I called!" I countered, raising my voice.

Austin steered the car onto a little gravel road off the side of the highway and threw it into park. I felt him looking at me, but I avoided eye contact.

"Your life hangs in the balance too," he said. "You saw how quickly Valerie turned on you when you went into Mike's room last night. If you say or do anything to make her think you're siding with Warren, she'll do it again."

"I won't let you do this," I said through gritted teeth as I got out of the car.

"Ava," he began, but I slammed the door shut, cutting off whatever else he was trying to say.

Keeping my eye on the horizon, I started walking briskly down the gravel road. The heavy rainfall had me drenched within seconds, but I didn't care. I needed a moment to myself—to calm down and clear my head before I said something I'd regret. I hated myself for yelling at him and storming off, but I'd hate myself even more if

I went along with his plan and things took a turn for the worse. Tears mixed with the rain running down my face as the thought of losing him hit me like a ton of bricks.

"Ava!" Austin yelled after me.

I heard the slamming of a car door and footsteps quickly approaching me from behind. Then a strong, steady hand grasped my arm and spun me around.

"What?" I asked angrily.

His clothes were already soaked through, clinging tight to his athletic figure. Water dripped steadily from his hair and face.

"Look, we both went into the line of work for a reason," he said, still holding my arm tightly as if I were a flight risk. "Even though our lives are at risk sometimes, we're here to help others. We're like guardians of the paranormal world or something."

"Then let me face the danger alone," I said, yanking my arm from his grasp and taking a couple of steps back. "It won't do the world any good to have two dead guardians."

"If you go down, I'm going down with you," he said stubbornly.

"It's not like we haven't gone our separate ways during a case before," I reminded him. "Why are you fighting against this so much?"

"I'm just trying to protect you."

"Well don't," I snapped. My words came out harsher than I'd intended, but I was just so frustrated with him. "I did this stuff on my own just fine before I met you. Clearly I can take care of myself."

Austin ran his fingers through his soaking wet hair in frustration. Then he met my steady gaze. "I'm not going to stop protecting you. I don't care what you say."

"You should, because I'm not worth the risk," I blurted.

Despite the tension between us, that adorable grin of his came across his face, and a wave of calmness swept over me. He took a couple of steps closer. My heart stumbled over itself as he reached one hand out to hold mine—his touch melting everything inside me.

"Not worth the risk?" he repeated in disbelief. "You're worth *everything*."

"I-I am?" I stammered.

"Ava," he started in a low voice that made my insides tingle. "When are you going to realize that I love you?"

CHAPTER NINETEEN

His words made my stomach drop so hard it felt like I'd missed a step on a staircase. My thoughts screeched to a halt. I stared at him—mouth gaping open unattractively—trying to form a response but coming up blank.

"Y-You what?" I managed to ask.

He let out a soft chuckle. "You heard me."

Then he dropped my hand, turned away, and headed back to the car. I remained frozen in place, trying to get my brain to function properly again. Just when I started to realize he had feelings for me too, he went and stepped up his game. Of course I liked him… *a lot…* but did I love him?

Sam is going to have a heyday with this one.

I mentally shook myself and found the ability to walk back to the car. Austin maneuvered the car back onto the highway and we finished our trip in silence. Somehow I managed to get a little more shuteye along the way.

The sound of gravel grinding under the tires woke me up. A sinister feeling had settled around me, letting me know we'd arrived back at The Foster House. It was no longer raining, but I could tell by the sound of water splashing under the car that it had rained while we were gone. Clouds blocked out the light from the setting sun, leaving the bed-and-breakfast towering eerily in the darkness.

Once Austin parked the car, he looked over at me.

"Feeling better?" he asked gently.

I sighed and glanced down at my lap. "I won't feel any better until all of this is over."

We got out of the car and made our way inside, where we were greeted by an overly excited Sam. My heart dropped knowing I'd have to be the bearer of bad news. Our attempt to solve the world's problems had failed.

"How was your trip?" she asked hopefully.

"Fantastic," I grumbled.

Austin stood behind me and placed a hand on my shoulder. "It didn't go quite as planned."

Sam's face fell with the news, then she managed a small half-smile. "Well, did you learn anything new at least?"

"Yeah. We learned what really happened which is actually very helpful," Austin said. "Let's go upstairs and I'll play the recording for you."

In the privacy of our room, Austin pulled out the recorder for Sam to hear the entire conversation we had with Warren. The moment I heard his voice, I felt the anger rising inside me again. Grabbing some clean (and most importantly dry) clothes from my duffle bag, I went to take a shower to ease my mind.

I stood there, letting the warm water wash my cares away. For a moment I felt better—more relaxed. My mind was almost completely at peace. When the water turned lukewarm, I reluctantly got out. After drying off, I threw on a pair of pajamas and stepped out into the bedroom.

Unfortunately, the recording was still playing.

I walked over to the window and rested my head against it, feeling the cool night air through the glass. Somehow, despite knowing what lurked in those woods, gazing out into the darkness was keeping me calm and collected.

When are you going to realize that I love you?

Austin's words floated through my mind. My lips twitched upward in an attempt to smile. Focusing on that memory allowed me to tune out everything else going on in the room. I still couldn't believe he said those words.

Have I just been completely oblivious to his feelings for that long?

I thought about all the times I'd be worried or upset and he'd do just about anything to make me smile. The way he would put a hand on my shoulder or lightly touch my arm when assuring me everything would be okay.

The countless paranormal stakeouts where he'd show up with coffee for both of us, claiming he "just happened to grab an extra."

All those times he would tag along on cases just to make sure I was safe—even if it meant driving to another state in the middle of the night.

And the way he always looked at me with those sparkling ocean-blue eyes so filled with joy and adoration and… and *love*.

I closed my eyes and let out a soft breath. God, I was an idiot. How did I not see any of this before?

"How does Warren's version help?" Sam's voice interrupted my thoughts, pulling my attention back to the present.

Austin gave her a brief rundown on what we believed was happening—how spirits see things in black or white and the possibility of Valerie's memory being distorted by the wine.

Then Sam said, "Okay, so now what happens?"

"Since Warren won't do anything, Ava and I are going to confront Valerie ourselves," Austin said.

"What? When?" Sam sounded as shocked as I was worried.

"Tomorrow," he replied without hesitation.

Silence fell over the room. I kept my gaze focused on the darkness outside. I could feel them looking at me, as if waiting for me to react in some way, but I remained silent. Arguing had already proven to be useless, and I had nothing good to say about the matter. So why say anything at all?

"Neither of you need to risk your lives for us," Sam said finally. "We can just shut this place down and leave like everyone else did."

"I wondered if you might come to that conclusion," Austin admitted. "But Ava has been right all along. It's important for us to put Valerie's spirit to rest."

"Why?"

"You guys can leave, but eventually someone else will come here," he explained. "As long as she remains trapped here, innocent people will be at risk. It's no longer just about protecting your family. It's about protecting everyone."

"Oh. I see," she said quietly. After a moment she added, "Well, I guess I should get some rest. It sounds like you two should get some sleep too."

"We will," Austin assured her. "Goodnight."

I heard footsteps cross the room and then a door shut. The floor creaked as Austin approached me. His warm, familiar arms wrapped around my waist from behind, making my pulse accelerate against my will.

"Ava," he murmured softly, resting his chin on my shoulder. "I know you don't want any of this, but we came here to do a job. Let's not make things worse by arguing."

I sighed and allowed my body to relax against his. In that moment I realized how much I enjoyed being in his arms.

"I just want this to be done so we can go home."

"Me too," he whispered.

Then his arms tightened around me briefly before—unfortunately—letting go.

I turned around in time to see him snatch up a pair of pajama pants and head into the bathroom. Before closing the door, he looked back at me.

"This plan will work," he said. "I promise."

Once he disappeared into the bathroom, I walked over to the bed. A feeling of comfort surrounded me as I burrowed under the blankets. I had to force myself to think happy thoughts—which was easier said than done.

I had just started to drift off to dreamland when I felt the bed move slightly as Austin crawled in. He shifted a little closer and rested a hand on my side. It took every ounce of energy I had left in me to pretend to be asleep and not allow my body to react to his touch.

Then he placed a gentle kiss on the side of my head before rolling away.

I couldn't hide the smile on my face, but it didn't last long before exhaustion finally took over and I was dead to the world.

CHAPTER TWENTY

When I opened my eyes again, the room was filled with beautiful sunlight flooding in through the window. I rolled onto my back and stretched, letting out a sleepy sigh.

Then panic hit me when I realized I was alone.

"Austin!" I called out as I sat bolt upright.

"Hey." His casual reply came from the desk in the corner.

I sighed with relief, resting a hand over my racing heart. "Don't do that."

"Do what?"

"Disappear with a predator on the loose," I grumbled.

He spun the chair around to face me, laughing. "Do you have any idea what time it is?"

"No," I said, snatching my phone off the nightstand to check. My eyes widened. "It's after twelve o'clock! Why didn't you wake me earlier?"

"You needed the rest," he said simply. I started to argue against it, but he continued. "It's important for what we have planned today."

My heart dropped into my stomach as I remembered *The Plan*. Crap. I wasn't prepared for it at all.

As I got ready for the day, I wracked my brain for ways to persuade Austin to let me do the dirty work on my own. Every idea was discarded the moment it formed. I knew him too well—he would never agree to any of them.

"What are we bringing out there?" I asked.

"Nothing," he said.

I looked at him like he'd grown three heads. It was highly unusual for us to approach any paranormal encounters without at least an EMF meter or a video camera.

Sensing my confusion, he said, "We can already see Valerie. Anything we bring would just weigh us down if we needed to make a quick escape."

Translation: You know she's going to try to kill you.

Instead of sharing my thoughts out loud, I just nodded and kept my mouth shut.

We went downstairs and found Sam and Mike standing in front of the desk talking quietly. Once they saw us approaching, they fell silent and turned their attention to us.

"Samantha filled me in first thing this morning," Mike said, looking concerned. "Are you sure this is a good idea?"

"I've been back and forth about it," I muttered, giving Austin a disapproving side glance.

He ignored me and said, "We have to give it a shot. We have no other option since Warren refused to come here himself."

"Well, I wish you the best of luck," Mike said, glancing uneasily at the window that looked out toward the woods.

"I'm coming with you," Sam blurted suddenly.

We all turned to look at her.

I was getting ready to kindly—but firmly—reject her offer when I noticed she was wearing old, ripped jeans and a T-shirt rather than her usual business attire.

This wasn't a spur-of-the-moment decision. She had actually thought it through.

There was no stopping her.

"No," Mike said firmly.

"I'm an adult. You can't stop me," Sam informed him.

"I won't let you risk your life like this."

"Dad," Sam started, looking him square in the eyes. "You put yourself through all of this to be here for me. Now it's my turn to be there for you."

Mike hugged his daughter tightly as a single tear rolled down his cheek.

My heart squeezed painfully at the sight, and I had to blink back tears of my own. Austin grabbed my arm and quietly led me outside, giving them a moment alone.

"You know if something happens out there, Sam's safety is top priority," Austin said the moment the door clicked shut behind us.

"I know," I replied quietly.

A knot formed in my stomach. Because I knew exactly what he meant.

If something went wrong, I'd have to choose her over him.

He wrapped me in a warm embrace, sensing my worry. I clung to him a second longer than usual, silently praying it wouldn't be the last time.

The door suddenly opened behind us, making us jump apart.

"I'm ready," Sam said, stepping out to join us.

The three of us walked up to the edge of the woods and stopped.

I turned to look at Austin, hesitant to move forward with the plan. Letting him continue with us didn't feel right, but I knew he wouldn't listen to me if I told him to go back inside. Even if I decided to back out myself, he would do it without me.

I glanced back at The Foster House and spotted Mike watching us from the common room window. Even from this distance I could make out the reassuring thumbs-up he was giving me.

"Are you ready?" Austin asked.

I swallowed hard.

"I swear if anything happens to you…"

"I'll be fine," he said for what felt like the millionth time. Yet I still didn't believe him. "I promise."

I slowly stepped into the woods with Sam and Austin following close behind. The only sound was our feet sloshing through the mud left by the rain. The forest felt unnaturally quiet, as if the wildlife itself knew better than to linger here.

We walked until we came to the clearing where Sam and I had approached Valerie just a couple of days before.

Rays of bright sunlight shone straight down into the clearing, illuminating everything around us. Light glistened off of the water droplets resting on the leaves and blades of grass. It would've been beautiful if not for the heavy darkness lingering in the air.

I continued walking until I reached the center of the clearing. Then I turned to face my friends.

They had stopped at the edge of the clearing near the trees. Sam stood protectively in front of Austin, as if she were a human shield, almost completely blocking him from my view.

She gave me a tight nod, letting me know they were ready.

Taking a deep breath, I turned back toward the forest.

"Valerie!" I called out.

No response.

"Valerie, I need to talk to you!"

Still nothing.

Deciding I'd have to cut straight to the point to lure the dead girl to me, I said, "I found Warren."

A twig snapped behind me and I spun around to face the sound. Sam looked at me apologetically as she mouthed *sorry*.

When I turned back around, I jumped and let out a small squeak.

Valerie was now standing a couple of feet in front of me, looking like her true dead self. Her dark, sunken eyes bored into mine.

"I tried to get Warren to come here like you wanted, but he refused," I told her. "But he told me the whole story about the night you died. I think you'll finally find peace when you hear it."

Valerie stared at me without blinking. Her stillness concerned me—like the calm before a storm.

"You had a lot of wine that night—you were drunk. I think it affected your memory of what happened,"I said.

She tilted her head slightly, her brow creasing with confusion.

The thought of ending the conversation and hightailing it out of there crossed my mind.

No.

I won't leave this family behind too.

I knew if I left now, regret would follow me. There were too many lives at stake. I refused to let myself be a selfish coward like Warren.

"Warren rejected sex with you out of respect. When he did, you got mad. I'm sure you wouldn't have normally, but the wine..." My words trailed off as Valerie's eyes narrowed.

I felt the energy around her shift.

She was getting angry. I couldn't tell if it was directed toward me or the story her fiancé claimed to be true.

Keeping my voice steady, I continued. "He had no choice but to stop you."

A low growl escaped her as her fists clenched by her side. The more I spoke, the angrier she was becoming.

My heart pounded as fear creeped into me.

Despite every instinct screaming at me to shut up, I opened my mouth to speak again.

"Valerie and I were high school sweethearts..."

Warren's recorded voice blasted from behind me, replacing the sound of my own.

I spun around to see Austin holding the recorder in his hand. He had stepped around Sam, leaving himself fully exposed.

"She's telling the truth," Austin said.

Pure hatred filled Valerie's face as she looked past me at him. The young man she'd been okay with before had instantly become her newest enemy the second he sided with the man she believed had killed her.

She stepped around me and made a beeline for him.

Sam staggered backward away from him. I was relieved to see her back down from the impending danger.

Austin didn't budge as Valerie sped toward him. She snatched the recorder from his hand and snapped it in half like a twig, putting an end to Warren's story.

For a moment, relief washed over me. That was all she wanted.

But I was wrong.

The surprise on Austin's face vanished, replaced with absolute terror. I'd never seen him look that scared.

Valerie raised her hand and flicked her wrist.

An invisible force hurled Austin backward. He landed on his back with a heavy *thud!* The impact knocked the breath out of him.

Grimacing in pain, he rolled over and tried to stand. But Valerie grabbed his ankles with her death grip, preventing him from going anywhere.

"Ava, help!" Austin cried as Valerie began to drag him past me and deeper into the woods.

I wanted to help, but my body refused to move. Everything had taken such a sudden turn that my brain couldn't process it fast enough.

"Ava!" he shouted again.

Sam suddenly appeared in front of me, grabbing my shoulders and shaking me.

"Ava! Don't just stand there! She's going to kill him!"

She's going to kill him.

Those words shattered the paralysis.

I snapped back to reality and looked at Austin, who had grabbed a tree root sticking up from the ground, clinging to it desperately.

"Leave him alone!" I demanded. "He didn't do anything to you!"

As Valerie looked up at me, her grip loosened just enough for Austin to free himself.

"You can't keep doing this, Valerie. This has to stop!"

As I spoke, Sam ran over to Austin and tried to help him get to his feet. But Valerie's attention quickly returned to her escaping victim. She glared at Sam and let out a loud, almost demonic growl, causing Sam to retreat back to the edge of the clearing.

Valerie turned back to Austin, who was scrambling to stand. In one swift motion, she reached down and wrapped a hand firmly around his throat. His face turned red within seconds as his lungs begged for oxygen.

Adrenaline and rage surged through me. From that moment on, time seemed to slow down, making everything that happened next feel like hours rather than seconds.

"Let him go!" I screamed as I ran toward the dead girl.

Just as I prepared to tackle her, Valerie turned toward me, still gripping Austin's throat, and flashed me a dangerous look that made me stop dead in my tracks.

Before I could react, her invisible force flung me backward. My body skidded across the wet ground until I slammed into a large tree several yards away.

"Oh my god!" Sam cried from a distance.

Pain radiated through my body as I lay there, struggling to catch my breath. Once I made sure nothing was broken, I pulled myself upright. A cool breeze caressed my skin where the ground had torn through my clothes. Warm liquid trickled down my face. Using the back of my hand, I wiped it away.

Blood.

By the time I regained my bearings, Valerie had stopped choking Austin, but he was still gasping for air and looked ready to pass out. The dead girl straddled him, pinning him to the ground at the far end of the clearing. His weakened state left him no match for her as she violently ripped at his clothes, leaving lines of blood across his skin.

Sam was crouched at the base of a tree, shaking and sobbing uncontrollably. I wished she could help, but at least she was keeping herself safe.

I turned my attention back to Austin and instantly knew I was fighting a losing battle

But he meant more to me than anything.

He had always protected me.

Now it was my turn.

I got to my feet, trying not to alert Valerie. The adrenaline still pumping through my veins dulled the pain as I grabbed a large stick and quietly approached Valerie from behind.

Austin was watching me closely, pain and fear filling his face as Valerie continued to hurt him. If she heard me approach, she showed no sign of it.

Bloody lacerations covered his face and torso. Tears mixed with the blood as they streamed down his cheeks.

Seeing him like that—knowing he was here because of me—felt like my heart was caving in on itself.

I would have done anything to take his place so he wouldn't have to suffer.

I looked at the stick in my hand. There was no guarantee it would work, but I was willing to try anything to save him.

I raised the stick, preparing to swing.

Austin gave a slight shake of his head.

My grip loosened and the stick fell from my hand as the harsh reality of the situation set in.

There was nothing anyone could do.

Valerie wasn't going to give him a choice. She had already made the decision for him.

Tears poured from my eyes, stinging the cuts on my face, as the horrifying realization settled in that Austin—my best friend—was going to die.

Suddenly, a familiar voice boomed from behind us.

"Leave the boy alone, Valerie!"

CHAPTER TWENTY-ONE

Valerie's head snapped up at the sound of his voice as she stared into the distance. Following her gaze, I saw who the voice belonged to and my mouth flopped open in total surprise.

Warren Williams was approaching the scene with Mike trailing close behind.

Upon seeing a very distressed Sam, Mike rushed over to comfort his daughter who was still hunkered down at the base of the tree.

Valerie rose to her feet and stumbled a few steps back. I quickly stepped off to the side before she could collide into me. Several emotions flickered across her face all at once—the strongest being shock. The entire area fell silent as we all stared at the dead girl, wondering what her next move would be.

Warren hobbled across the clearing and stopped beside Austin, putting maybe five feet between Valerie and himself. Although her body tensed up, I was surprised to see she wasn't running away or attacking the old man.

Instead, she stood still as a statue, looking her fiancé square in the eyes.

"I never meant for this to happen," Warren said quietly. His voice trembled with sadness.

Valerie didn't move a muscle.

"You don't really remember that night, do you?"

Valerie's shoulders slumped forward as she lowered her gaze. It was as if she realized I'd been right earlier—the wine had messed with her memory.

"Well, I do. Very clearly," Warren said.

Tears streamed down his face as he repeated the story of that tragic night to his dead lover. As he spoke, I kept waiting for her to lash out again—to scream, to attack him, to do something.

But she didn't.

She remained rooted in place, listening.

Maybe she was still in shock of seeing him, or maybe she was only willing to hear the truth from him and no one else. Whatever the reason, I was grateful Austin was still alive and no further harm was being done.

"I thought you were dead," Warren finished, his voice cracking. "If I'd known you weren't..."

His eyes landed on me.

"I'm sorry for everything. I should've never run away, and I should've come back with you when I had the chance."

When he turned back to Valerie, his face softened, but his next words were laced with disappointment and anger.

"But look what you've done, Valerie!" He waved a hand toward Austin. "You've harmed so many people—taken innocent lives—and for what? For a mistake that *I* made years ago. This has to stop."

Valerie hung her head in shame.

"I wanted to spend the rest of my life with you, Val," Warren continued, his voice softening again. "I loved you then, and I still love you now."

I knew it was impossible, but I swear tears shimmered in Valerie's eyes as she looked at him.

"But please stop hurting everyone else. I'm the one you want—not my family and certainly not this innocent boy."

Valerie took small, hesitant steps toward Warren, closing the distance between them.

We all exchanged worried looks. I braced myself for the worst.

Then something incredible happened.

As if time itself were reversing, Valerie began to change right before our eyes. Her decayed flesh smoothed and healed. The wounds disappeared. The hollow darkness faded from her eyes.

The corpse vanished.

In its place stood the beautiful young woman she once was.

She was fully clothed, wearing the same white cocktail dress from the photo I'd seen of her and Warren. Her dark, silky hair flowed behind her in the gentle breeze. Her once-dead eyes now shone a deep forest green, though sorrow and regret lingered in them.

Warren's eyes widened in awe.

Then Valerie turned away from him and walked over toward Mike and Sam.

They slowly stood as she approached, and Mike stepped in front of his daughter protectively. But calmness radiated from Valerie now—so different from the rage she'd shown moments earlier—that I felt certain of my next words.

"She won't hurt you," I said.

Valerie rested a hand on Mike's arm. A smile formed on his face and I saw his mouth move, though I couldn't hear what he was saying. Then she looked at Sam and nodded once before turning away.

Her gaze settled on me.

Even though she no longer seemed dangerous, a flicker of panic still rose in my chest as she approached. When she wrapped her ice-cold arms around me, I froze for a moment before slowly returning the unexpected hug.

Thank you for helping me.

Her words whispered softly through my mind. I couldn't help but smile.

She stepped back and glanced between Austin and me—Austin still sitting on the ground, propped up on his elbows. A knowing smile crossed her face as if she could see straight through us and into everything we felt.

Then she turned back to Warren.

"I love you, Val," Warren said.

She lifted a hand to caress his cheek. Judging by the smile on his face, I knew she'd used her telepathy to answer him. Then she stood on her tiptoes and kissed him softly.

Afterward, she looked at all of us, her voice drifting through our minds.

I'm sorry for everything. Please forgive me.

Her body began to shimmer as she slowly lifted into the air. Suddenly a brilliant ball of light burst around her, illuminating the entire clearing.

Then she was gone.

"Is it over?" Sam asked hesitantly.

"Yes," I said with relief. "She learned the truth, realized what she'd done, and finally found peace with her own death. She's moved on."

Sam and Mike hugged each other tightly as tears of joy slid down their faces. Then they walked over to Warren, who was sobbing uncontrollably.

"Let's get you back inside," Mike said gently, placing a hand on Warren's shoulder.

Together, the three of them headed toward The Foster House. Sam stopped to look back at Austin and me, chewing nervously on her bottom lip.

"Don't worry, we'll be there shortly," I assured her.

"Are you sure?" she asked.

"Positive."

She nodded and continued onward.

The adrenaline had worn off, and pain began radiating throughout my body as I walked toward Austin. I offered him a hand as he slowly—and painfully, judging by the sounds he made—got back on his feet.

Bruises had already begun to appear on his neck where Valerie had choked him. His ripped clothes left parts of his legs and most of his torso exposed. Bloody lacerations and mud covered nearly every inch of him.

He looked every bit like a hot, badass warrior.

"Are you okay?" he asked.

"That depends," I said cautiously. "You're not going to die, are you?"

"No, I'm not."

"Then yeah, I'm okay," I said. "Just a little banged up."

He studied me carefully, concern—and a little frustration—written all over his face. "Why did you do that anyway?"

"Do what?"

"Try to attack Valerie," he said, his voice accusing. "You knew the strength she possessed. You could've been killed."

I threw my arms out in exasperation. "I was trying to save your life!"

"I knew what I was getting myself into," he countered. "Anything that happened was my own fault. You didn't need to save me."

"I would've done *anything* to be in your place!" I blurted, my voice rising as tears threatened to escape.

His head jerked back in surprise.

"I would've died to save you, Austin. Do you have any idea how much you mean to me?"

He rubbed the back of his neck as he struggled to find the right words.

"Well, I, uh..."

I shook my head in amusement and ran a hand through my hair—unintentionally mimicking Austin's usual nervous habit. The corners of my mouth tilted up into a wide smile, and a bubble of laughter escaped me as the realization hit.

"What?" he asked, confused by my strange elation.

"Austin," I began. "When are you going to realize that I love you too?"

A gigantic smile spread across his face, sending my heart racing.

I opened my mouth to say something else—probably to start rambling—but he didn't give me the chance. In one smooth motion, he closed the distance between us, sliding one hand around my waist and pulling me against him. With the other hand, he lifted my chin and kissed me.

It started off gentle.

Then it deepened.

Warm electricity shot through my entire body, making every nerve come alive.

For that moment, it felt like we were the only two people in the world. Everything that had happened over the past few days—the fear, the chaos, the danger— faded away.

The kiss ended far too soon, leaving us both breathing a little harder. I looked into Austin's eyes. The pain that had been there earlier was gone, replaced with happiness and love.

We smiled at each other.

Then he gently kissed my forehead.

"You have no idea how long I've waited to do that," he said.

He stepped beside me, wrapping one arm around my waist.

"Come on. Let's go inside."

Together, we made our way back to The Foster House.

* * * *

Sam, Mike, and Warren were all sitting on the sofa talking when we stepped into the lobby. The three of them immediately stood when they saw us.

"I knew it!" Sam exclaimed when she spotted Austin's arm around me.

I rolled my eyes while Austin chuckled and pulled me a little closer.

"So it's really over?" Mike asked.

"Yes, sir," Austin replied.

"I can't thank you enough for all of this," Sam said.

I nodded toward Warren. "He's the one you should be thanking. All we did was find him. But he's the real hero."

"You saved my life," Austin said sincerely. "Thank you."

Warren's eyes filled with tears again at the unexpected praise.

"I just wish I'd come back sooner,"he admitted.

"Better late than never," Austin said. After a moment, he added, "What made you decide to come back?"

"When Mike found out what you planned to do, he tracked down my phone number and called me," Warren explained. "Hearing my own family begging for help touched something in me. I realized it was time."

Mike patted him on the shoulder. "I'm glad you came to your senses, old man."

"It was hard, but it was the right thing to do."

"Well, if you don't mind, we're going to get our stuff and get out of your hair," Austin said.

Upstairs, we changed into clean clothes and gathered our belongings. Mike let us into his room—which had returned to a normal temperature—to retrieve our hidden cameras. Once everything was ready to go, we gathered in the lobby to say our goodbyes.

Mike offered for us to come stay again anytime we wanted—free of charge. Sam handed us a check for the amount due along with a little extra as a thank you for everything.

After agreeing to keep in touch, we all exchanged hugs and handshakes before stepping outside the now peaceful bed-and-breakfast.

Austin and I tossed our bags into our vehicles. Then he walked over and kissed me again.

"Are you ready?" he asked.

I nodded enthusiastically.

"Let's go home."

EPILOGUE

It was near the end of October—five months since Austin and I worked the case at The Foster House. After Valerie's spirit found peace, Warren turned himself in to the police and a trial date was set for December ninth.

After Valerie's spirit found peace, Warren turned himself in to the police and a trial date was set for December ninth. The story hit the news all across the nation. As word spread, Mike and Sam began receiving donations to build a memorial for Valerie.

It had finally been unveiled a week ago, but Austin and I were working another case and couldn't attend the big event.

So now we were on our way to Arkansas to see it for ourselves.

Mike and Sam had become advocates for male domestic violence. If it wasn't for the stigma toward men who are abused, Warren may have sought help immediately and Valerie might still be alive today. Though the abusive situation had only happened once between them, being drunk was no excuse for Valerie's actions. One terrible mistake quickly led to another, costing people their lives in the end.

In other news, our careers as paranormal investigators had taken off after word spread about us solving The Foster House case. Austin and I combined our businesses and were taking on more—and bigger—cases than ever before.

"I can't believe Warren died in his sleep last night," I said to Austin as we approached the driveway to The Foster House. "It kind of makes me wonder if I took the case and almost got you killed for no reason."

"His death wouldn't have solved anything," he said calmly. Then he glanced at me, grinning, and reached over to take my hand. "And I wouldn't say it was all for nothing. We both got something pretty amazing out of it."

I smiled back as he turned the car into the driveway.

It was our first time back since May.

Relief washed over me as I noted the eerie sensation that had once hung over the property was completely gone. The bed-and-breakfast came into view, and the parking lot was packed. Off in the distance near the woods, a group of people was gathered around Valerie's memorial.

Austin managed to squeeze the Lexus into one of the few remaining spaces in the small lot. As we stepped out of the car, I heard footsteps approaching.

"Hey guys!" Sam greeted us as she hurried over and wrapped me in a big, sisterly hug.

Mike appeared beside her and smiled warmly. "It's good to see you crazy kids again."

"It's nice to be back," I said.

"As long as I'm not going to almost die again," Austin joked, earning a round of laughter from all of us.

We grabbed our belongings from the car and followed Mike and Sam inside. Everything looked exactly the same as it had before, but the peaceful, welcoming feeling surrounding the place made it feel like an entirely new building.

We were assigned to the same room we stayed in before, which instantly made us feel right at home.

"We have exciting news!" Sam gushed when Austin and I returned to the lobby a few minutes later. "Dad got a letter in the mail yesterday approving his plans to open two new centers for male victims of domestic violence right here in Arkansas."

"That's fantastic!" I exclaimed.

"Congratulations," Austin said.

"Thank you." Mike said proudly, practically beaming.

"Are you ready to see the memorial?" Sam asked.

I nodded excitedly. The four of us headed outside. The group of people that had been gathered near the woods earlier had already dispersed, leaving the area quiet again.

As we approached the tree line, flashbacks from the last time we stood there—the day we confronted Valerie—flooded my mind. My steps slowed until I finally stopped altogether.

"Babe, it's okay," Austin assured me gently. "Everything is fine now. I'm not in danger this time—nobody is."

"I know," I said quietly. "It's just hard to think about that day."

"I know." He kissed my forehead and squeezed my hand reassuringly. "But it's over."

With his hand wrapped firmly around mine, we continued walking.

When we reached the memorial, my eyes widened in awe.

The tall marble slab had Valerie's name engraved in large letters, along with her birth and death dates. Above the engraving was a blown-up version of the photo I'd found of her and Warren at their high school prom.

Along the base of the memorial was a little ledge filled with flowers and little mementos that visitors had left behind.

"It's beautiful!" I said softly.

"I want to get a picture of you two beside it," Sam said. "After all, you both helped make this happen."

Austin wrapped his arm around my waist and we stood beside the memorial. Sam pulled out her phone and snapped a photo.

"I'll text it to you so you can have it," she said.

A moment later, my phone chimed.

I opened the image she had sent and froze.

Chills ran down my spine as I stared at the screen.

Austin and I stood beside the memorial, his arm around my waist just like I remembered.

But we weren't alone in the picture.

On the other side of the memorial was the faint, ghostly image of Valerie and Warren—young, happy, and alive as ever.

Holding each other in an eternal embrace.

The End

LOVED THIS BOOK?
SUPPORT THE AUTHOR BY LEAVING A REVIEW!

CHAPTER ONE

The sound of teeth chattering pulled my attention away from the closed door. Carrie Johnson stood next to me, her clammy hand grasping my arm as if her life depended on it — which it might. She'd moved in a few weeks ago with her husband, Nathan, and their twin toddlers, Allie and Riley. I received an email from Carrie two days ago asking me to get rid of a poltergeist that had been causing too much chaos for her liking.

Now here we stood: Carrie pallid and violently shaking, looking ready to bolt at any moment, and me, trying my best to remain calm and collected. On the inside, I was screaming like a scared little girl. Needless to say, this was no poltergeist — my mere presence appeared to anger it even more.

I took a deep, calming breath as I slowly opened the door. The musty scent of the cellar replaced the sweet aroma of Carrie's floral perfume. Although I saw nothing but darkness as I peered down the stairs, I knew he was down there. The steady creaking of old wood drifted up to us eerily, instantly raising the hair on the nape of my neck.

"Y-you're not going down there, are you?" Carrie

whispered shakily. I flinched ever so slightly as her fingernails dug into my arm.

I nodded as I held a finger up to my lips. Her frightened brown eyes were begging me to not go. I motioned for her to stay put before carefully placing my foot on the first step.

The loose wooden step creaked under my foot. Damn these old houses, I thought. There was no way I'd make it down without being heard. Hesitantly, I took the next step, then another, and another. Although I reached the bottom of the old, janky staircase within seconds, it felt much longer.

The steady creaking sound continued, louder now. I looked straight ahead and squinted, but it was too dark to see anything. The light switch was at the top of the stairs, but I'd decided against turning it on in fear of giving away my presence. I'm sure the stairs took care of that. I rolled my eyes at the thought.

Figuring my presence was already well-known, I pulled my cell phone out of my back pocket to use as a flashlight. Keeping the light aimed toward the ground, I tiptoed forward. As I walked deeper into the cellar, another sound joined the creaking: humming.

I listened intently, trying to make out the tune. It wasn't anything I recognized — if it was even a real song at all. I took a few more baby steps forward then stopped. Trying to will my hand to stop shaking, I slowly aimed the light straight ahead.

There he was — moving back and forth in an old rocking chair, his back to me. His jet-black hair was sticking out in every direction. Through the back of the chair, I could tell he still had on the button-down shirt and slacks he wore to work earlier in the day. He continued humming his tune, seemingly unaware that I was standing no more than six feet away.

"Nathan?" My voice cracked as I called his name.

Carrie's husband continued to rock and hum. I racked my brain for something that would capture his attention.

"Allie and Riley are waiting for you to tuck them in." It was a lie, but any father in their right mind would immediately react to their children wanting them.

But Nathan didn't.

That isn't Nathan. The words drifted through my mind unexpectedly, making me gasp in surprise. Although I couldn't see his face, I knew for a fact this man was Nathan. I already had searched the house from top to bottom. Only the four family members resided here. Who else could it be?

Then I had a chilling realization. It was Nathan on the outside. . .but maybe someone else was on the inside. Instantly, I knew what to say next. I took a deep, shaky breath as I prepared to speak the Latin exorcism prayer that I'd memorized a few months prior.

"Exorcizámos te, ómnis immúnde spiritus—"

My words were barely above a whisper, but Nathan's head whipped around in response and his black eyes bore into mine. I stumbled backward, heart pounding heavily as fear pulsed through me.

A sarcastic grin spread across his chiseled face. In a voice that was much deeper and raspier than his own, he said, "Sorry, Princess. That's not going to work on me."

"Ómnis satanic potéstas," I continued, ignoring him. Although I knew very little about demons, I was aware of the little tricks they liked to play to get out of being exorcised.

My words came to a halt as Nathan's mouth opened wide — so wide that I feared his skin would tear. Silence filled the room around us. Then suddenly Nathan let out a demonic roar that vibrated the air around me and sent his putrid breath flying in my direction.

I damn near dropped my phone as I spun around and bolted for the stairs, gagging and tripping over my own feet along the way. As soon as I reached the top, I slammed the door shut and locked it. Pushing past Carrie, I rushed into the living room and shoved my belongings into the two duffel bags I'd brought with me.

"What happened?" Carrie demanded, trailing me.

"He's possessed!" I shouted. I instantly felt bad for yelling at her, but fear and adrenaline made it difficult for me to be calm.

"What!" Her eyes widened in disbelief.

"Carrie, listen to me." I kept my eyes locked on hers, trying to convey the urgency through them. "You need to grab your kids and get out of here."

"But they're sleeping. . ."

"Now!"

Tears were streaming down her face, her bottom lip trembling. Pushing her dark brown bangs to the side, she ran a shaky hand across her forehead. "But he's my husband. I can't leave him behind."

"You have to," I stated firmly. "A demon is possessing his body, Carrie." I clenched and unclenched my jaw as my voice turned cold. "I'm sorry, but that's not your husband anymore."

"No!" she screamed in denial.

Without another word, I flung both duffel bags over my shoulder and made a beeline for the front door. I stepped out into the cool night. A thin layer of clouds covered the full moon, making the night appear even more sinister. I rushed toward my Jeep, which was parked at the end of the driveway.

"Ava!" Carrie's frightened voice came from behind me. "Please don't go. We need you!"

I swallowed the lump in my throat as I turned to tell her the truth. "I can't help you. I-I'm sorry," I stammered as tears threatened to spill out. "I've never been up against a demon before. I'm not good enough to deal with this on my own!"

"So you're just leaving us alone to die?" Her voice was thick with anger and a sense of betrayal.

Guilt slammed into me. I'd never walked out on a case before. But my life had never been in danger like this before either. Did choosing my life over theirs make me a coward? Probably. Perhaps a coward like me shouldn't be a paranormal investigator after all. . .

"Look, I have to get out of here and so should you." Before she could protest, I rambled on. "I'll find a local priest or someone who's better fit for exorcisms, but for now you have to leave."

I threw my bags in the Jeep and opened the driver's-side door.

"Ava, please," Carrie begged.

"I'm sorry," I muttered softly before climbing in and driving away.

I spared one last glance into the rearview mirror. Carrie was still standing at the end of the driveway, waving me down. My heart ached at the sight. It took only a second for me to realize I could no longer see the house because it was now shrouded by smoke as dark as the night sky.

I slammed the brakes and threw the Jeep into park. I jumped out and began to run back to the house, but came to a dead stop when a snake-like tendril reached out from the smoke toward Carrie. My mouth opened to tell her to run, but a bloodcurdling scream came out instead as the tendril wrapped around her body and yanked her backward into the smoky darkness.

GET IT NOW!

ABOUT THE AUTHOR

C. Smith is an author whose journey began in her hometown in Indiana and continues in her new home near the Great Smoky Mountains in Tennessee. With a lifelong passion for storytelling, she finds writing to be a therapeutic outlet, helping her navigate life as a neurodivergent individual.

The inspiration for her debut book came from a haunting nightmare that ignited the journey to turn a dream of becoming an author into reality. She hopes to continue down this path in hope of bringing the world together through the power of healing and connection that storytelling brings.